Logan wa

He reached out and slipped his arm beneath her, drawing her lush body against him. Although sharp desire coursed through him, he took his time, exploring the soft curve of her breast, the narrowness of her waist, the smooth length of her thigh.

When he could no longer resist, he brushed his lips against hers, teasing, tasting. Her lips were so soft, so moist. She sighed and pressed herself against him in invitation. His fingers lingered on her inner thigh and she opened up to him, welcoming his touch.

Giving in to his overwhelming need, he rose above her. His moan merged with hers. Mouth to mouth, flesh to flesh, they began to move as one. He could hear the sound of her breathing growing faster. Harder. He knew they were reaching the end of their journey. For a moment he fought against the speed, wanting the pleasure to go on. His mind struggled, trying to separate dream from reality.

But it was too late.

He felt her tighten convulsively around him, felt the shudders of pleasure shoot through her. As he lost himself in her, only one thought was clear.

This was no dream....

Dear Reader,

Writing *While He Was Sleeping* has been so much fun! Especially since it gave me a chance to tell Logan Campbell's story. He made my heart beat a little faster from the moment he appeared in my last Temptation, #700 *The Last Bachelor*. He was definitely a man of mystery. All I knew for certain was that he was a loner and he preferred it that way.

Of course, that got me wondering…what kind of heroine would be able to break down Logan's defenses and worm her way into his heart?

And that's how I discovered Daisy Hanover— a truly unpredictable heroine. She has such an active imagination that I could never tell what she was going to do next. And neither could Logan. From the moment he woke up beside her in a bed that claimed magical powers, he found her frustrating, exasperating…and totally captivating. One minute she was scaring the life out of him, and the next, she was making him laugh out loud. And in spite of all his wishes to the contrary, she stole her way into his heart—the same way she stole her way into his bed *While He Was Sleeping*.

I hope you have as much fun as I did getting to know this pair of mismatched lovers who discover the magic of true love.

Enjoy!

Carolyn Andrews

P.S. I love to hear from my readers. You can write to me at P.O. Box 327, DeWitt, NY 13214.

WHILE HE WAS SLEEPING
Carolyn Andrews

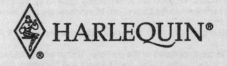

TORONTO • NEW YORK • LONDON
AMSTERDAM • PARIS • SYDNEY • HAMBURG
STOCKHOLM • ATHENS • TOKYO • MILAN • MADRID
PRAGUE • WARSAW • BUDAPEST • AUCKLAND

To my dad—Andrew A. Fulgenzi, M.D., my inspiration and my guide. You've always been there when I needed you. Happy Father's Day. I love you.
With special thanks to Mary Puthawala and Garda Parker, my fellow writers and critique partners, who helped me capture Logan and Daisy.

ISBN 0-373-25835-6

WHILE HE WAS SLEEPING

Copyright © 1999 by Carolyn Hanlon

1

"LOOKING FOR a romantic getaway with guaranteed results?"

Daisy Hanover clicked twice on her mouse, adjusted her glasses and leaned closer to her computer screen.

"Sleep in this bed once, and you and your lover will be soul mates forever!"

Could this be the answer to her prayer? Quickly she scanned the information on the colorful Web site.

A secluded cabin in the Catskills—one that boasted a bed with special powers. A bed, the site claimed, that for centuries had given the gift of true love to the couples lucky enough to sleep in it.

A magic bed?

Stories from her childhood swirled through Daisy's mind. *The Legend of Sleepy Hollow, Rip van Winkle.* Unusual things happened in the Catskills.

Quickly, she skimmed through the testimonials of satisfied customers, her eyes growing wider and wider. It was a special bed indeed that could promise both lasting love *and* great sex.

It might solve her problem in one fell swoop.

Her finger moved to the mouse to download all the information. Then suddenly she snatched her hand back.

Was she that big a ding-a-ling? Did she really think that a magic bed could make her suddenly fall in love with Phillip? Or make Phillip fall in love with her?

In her mind Daisy could picture the word *ding-a-ling* in neon letters over her head. Blinking on and off. She glanced down at her engagement ring. As she stared at it, it seemed to grow larger, heavier on her hand. In the two months since Phillip had placed it there, she'd felt as if a clock had started ticking off the minutes to doomsday. The ticking grew louder and louder until she pictured the neon letters over her head suddenly exploding into a million pieces.

Rising quickly, Daisy shook her head to rid it of the image, then circled the counter and began to pace in the limited space at the front of her bookstore. Why couldn't she be happy with what Phillip had offered her—a marriage based on friendship and respect? So what if there wasn't any special spark between them? Hadn't he been there for her while her Aunt Angela was dying...?

Daisy paused in front of the window, took off her glasses and stared out at the street. Even now, she didn't like to think about the difficult months that had preceded her aunt's death. Aunt Angela was the second mother she'd lost. When she was barely two, her mother and father had both been taken from her in a boating accident in the Caribbean. That was when Aunt Angela and Uncle Daniel had adopted her. Since then, her second family had meant everything to her, and when Phillip had first taken a job with Hanover Securities a little over a year ago, that family had been falling apart.

As her Aunt Angela's heart condition had worsened, Uncle Daniel had totally buried himself in work. He'd begun to stay overnight in Manhattan instead of commuting home, and her younger cousin Stevie had felt she was losing not only her mother, but her father too.

The first weekend that Uncle Daniel had brought Phillip, his new assistant, home to work with him, Phillip had asked Daisy what he could do to help.

After that, things had gotten better. Phillip would travel home with Daniel during the week so that they could work on the train. And it was Phillip who'd found a nurse to move into the house so that Daisy wasn't overburdened caring for her aunt.

Once more, Daisy gazed down at her engagement ring. She was very grateful to Phillip Baldwin. She respected him, admired him. The problem was, she didn't love him. Before she'd accepted his proposal of marriage, she'd been quite honest about that. And Phillip had told her how charmed he was by her candor, that a marriage based on honesty and friendship had a much greater chance of surviving than one based on such a transitory thing as love.

Even now, as she recalled the scene, Daisy could feel a little band of pain tighten around her heart. Phillip had gone on to enumerate the practical advantages of their marriage. He would gain a wife who would understand the demands of his career and help him to meet them. And she would ensure that her cousin Stevie had a stable home life during her teenage years.

The whole proposal was so...logical. And it had appealed to the practical Daisy Hanover, ex–research librarian-turned-bookstore owner. Daisy sighed. But there was another part of her that really would have preferred a very different kind of proposal. One that made her heart flutter.

"Flutter, schmutter," said the practical voice in her head. "You'd prefer to go into cardiac arrest? Remember that Phillip's proposal made your Aunt Angela very happy."

Daisy sighed again. She would be forever grateful to Phillip for easing at least one of her aunt's worries. And she could still recall Aunt Angela's words. "Phillip's a good man. He'll make a fine husband."

Why couldn't she be satisfied with that?

"Because," the logical voice in her head whispered, "you're just like your father."

No, she wasn't! If she were really like her father, she would break her engagement, take the money her aunt had left her in her will and run away. That's what her father had done. He'd sold his shares in Hanover Securities, left his brother to run the company alone and run away to marry the woman he loved. A woman his family had rejected because she was outside his social sphere.

She'd spent all of her life trying to make up to her uncle and aunt for her father's desertion. So she was not going to run away.

Turning from the window, Daisy glanced at the piles of books and articles that covered her desk. As a former research librarian, she knew how to gather information. And plenty had been written on the topic of making a man fall in love with you. Pushing her glasses back up on her nose, she strode purposefully toward the desk. Now all she had to do was sift through it and put it to use.

After that, she'd tackle step two—trying to make herself fall in love with Phillip. She had two weeks to the wedding. Daisy's gaze shifted to the computer. But if there was a magic bed…and *if* it worked…it just might be possible to kill two birds with one stone.

She sat down and studied the screen again, for the first time noticing the box in the upper right corner. History of the Bed, the headline read. Eagerly, she scrolled through the text. The inscription above the intertwining rings on the bed's headboard, it told her, was believed to be in an ancient Celtic language, and it was widely held that the bed could trace its special powers to Merlin. However, there were conflicting theories about how it had made its way to the New World.

Some believed that it had been brought by the Irish monks in their early voyages of discovery. Frowning, Daisy shook her head. *Wrong.* Several well-respected historians supported the theory that Irish monks led by Saint Brendan had indeed "discovered" America even before Leif Eriksson had. She'd even come across drawings of what their boats had looked like. They wouldn't have held a bed! Nor could she find it easy to believe that monks would have had anything to do with transporting a bed that was supposed to turn your lover into the kind of incredible, erotically satisfying expert you'd only dreamed about before.

No wonder the most widely preferred theory maintained that the bed had been magically transported to the Americas by Irish witches who could trace their heritage back to Merlin. As Daisy tried to picture this "magic transportation" in her mind, she couldn't suppress a grin. A sort of "Beam me up, Scotty," approach to furniture moving? How inventive, not to mention convenient.

And she'd done a lot of reading about Merlin. If the bed's magic could be traced to the magician, it might just be... *a special bed that acted as a love potion?*

Why not?

"Because," whispered the practical voice in Daisy's head, "if there were such a bed, someone would have stolen it years ago, slapped a patent on it, and one of the television shopping networks would be offering it on an easy-payment plan."

Right. Daisy leaned back in her chair. There couldn't be any such thing as a magic bed.

With a sigh, she lifted her gaze from the computer screen and looked around her store at the shelves of neatly stacked books. Each one was filled with an adventure. Adventures that pulled at her. But she was never going to experience any of them firsthand. Instead, she would marry Phillip and settle down to live a very practical, logical life.

She felt a wave of panic and longing wash over her.

Was this how her father had felt just before he had taken his inheritance and run away from the practical, logical life his family had mapped out for him?

Was she her father's daughter after all?

There were times when she knew it was true. There were even times when she imagined that she could hear her father's voice whispering to her, promising her that life was an adventure and that true love did exist. That it was worth searching for and finding. That it was the only real *magic.*

Daisy stared at the computer screen once more. Maybe it wasn't so ridiculous to think that it might be found in a magic bed.

"Don't be absurd!" said her practical side.

"Take a chance!" urged her romantic side.

"What would you think if I pierced my nose?" asked a voice from the other side of the counter.

Startled, Daisy nearly leaped out of her chair. Then, taking a deep breath, she turned to face her seventeen-year-old cousin. "I didn't hear you come in."

"You never hear anything when you're lost in research. I want to know what you'd think if I pierced my nose?"

Daisy barely prevented herself from wincing as she studied her cousin carefully. In the two months since her mother's death, Stephanie Ann Hanover had chopped off her Alice-in-Wonderland hair, dyed it bright red and changed her wardrobe from preppy-sophisticate to what her father called "rag-picker special." She'd even shed her name. Stephanie Ann had become Stevie.

"You really don't care what I'd think about it," Daisy said. "If you drill a hole through your nose, it will be because you want to shock your father."

With a sigh, Stevie whirled and threw herself in the nearest beanbag chair. "If I wanted to get Dad's attention, I'd have to do more than pierce my nose. I'd have to slit my wrists."

"I vote for piercing," Daisy said. "It won't leave nearly as big a scar as slicing your wrists."

Stevie's eyes narrowed. "You think I'm kidding?"

"I think that no matter how angry you are with your father, you're too smart to do something dangerous."

Stevie shrugged and hunkered down farther into the chair. "Yeah, well, my father doesn't share your faith in me. He's still insisting that I turn over all my inheritance money to him so that he can 'invest it wisely' for me. He doesn't believe I'm capable of doing that for myself. If I'd been a boy, he'd think differently. Then he'd want me to follow in his footsteps. But I'm going to prove him wrong."

Daisy bit back a sigh. The new will that her

Aunt Angela had written shortly before she died was only widening the rift between Stevie and her father. And Daisy wasn't sure how to put a stop to it. Thanks to her aunt's generosity, she and Stevie were each suddenly two million dollars richer. And Uncle Daniel was furious.

The inheritance made them "prime fortune hunters' bait," according to her uncle.

But Daisy suspected that the real reason Uncle Daniel was fit to be tied was that Aunt Angela had written the will behind his back. She'd even secretly hired a lawyer, a Mr. Maplethorpe, who had appeared on the doorstep a few days after the funeral with the will in hand. And it was perfectly legal, therefore negating Angela Hanover's earlier will, which would have required that Daisy and Stevie wait until they were thirty to get control of their inheritance.

There were times, like the present, when Daisy wished that her aunt had never changed her will. "I'm sure you'll handle the money wisely," she said.

"Well, I won't turn it over to my fiancé to invest for me the way you're doing. And I'm not going to turn it over to my father either. That's what Daddy would call handling it *wisely*." Stevie paused at Daisy's desk, and studied her. "Don't you ever get tired of doing the practical thing? Aren't you ever tempted to do something wild and exciting and romantic like your father did?"

"Don't romanticize my father, Stevie. He ran away from his family obligations."

"Yeah. But he never ran out on you. He made you a part of his life."

"Stevie, your father—"

"Don't try to make excuses for him," Stevie warned with a scowl. "He didn't have any time for Mom when she was dying. And as soon as I get my inheritance, he won't have any time for me either." Stevie reached for one of the books on Daisy's desk. "And you don't have to worry. I'm not going to slit my wrists. I have something much better in mind. Something that will make everybody sit up and take notice. Even you.... Whoa! Wait a minute. Just what are you researching here? *Fifty Ways to Please a Man?*" She picked up another book. "*Male Sexual Fantasies?* Oh, I get it. You're worried that Phillip's going to turn into a workaholic like my dad, aren't you?"

"I don't think that's any of—"

"You'd be better off surfing the Net for sex advice," Stevie said as she moved to the computer.

"Stevie..."

"Good grief." Stevie let out a low whistle. "I guess I don't have to tell a former research librarian about surfing the Net. Romance *and* great sex in the Catskills? Who would have thought?" Clicking the mouse, Stevie brought up a new screen, then giggled. "Look. They even claim George Washington slept in this bed."

"George Washington slept in so many beds it's a wonder he had time to be president," Daisy said.

"At least they claim he slept with Martha in this one."

Leaning over Stevie's shoulder, Daisy stared at the screen. "Maybe the bed does work. Could be that's why she put up with those wooden teeth."

Flipping to a new screen, Stevie scanned it quickly. "You know if you're really serious about attracting Phillip, I've heard about something that's supposed to work."

Daisy sent her a wary look.

"Pierce your tongue."

"Ouch!" Daisy winced.

"I'm serious. One of the girls at school did it. She says guys think it's cool. What do you think Phillip's reaction would be?"

"I'm trying very hard to picture it right now. I don't think *cool* describes it."

She and Stevie burst out laughing at the same time. They were still struggling for breath when the bell over the door jingled.

"That's not fair," Mark Dawson complained as he entered the store. "The two of you are having a great time, and I have to ruin it by reminding Stevie we're supposed to be having a math lesson. I stopped up at the house, and Delores said you were down here."

With a grimace, Stevie rose from the chair. "I haven't forgotten, even though I'd like to." Then she sent Daisy a mischievous wink. "Maybe you can help us out, Mark. Would you be attracted by a girl who pierced her tongue?"

For a moment Mark looked totally nonplussed, and Daisy couldn't help grinning. It wasn't easy for Stevie to put him off like that. Daisy judged him to be a few years her own senior, but he'd hit it off with her cousin from the day he'd started working at the house as Aunt Angela's nurse. And he'd won Daniel's everlasting gratitude when his efforts to tutor Stevie in math had transformed her grades from F's to A's. Since Angela's funeral, Mark had continued the tutoring sessions with Stevie on Friday afternoons.

"I advise taking the Fifth, Mark," Daisy suggested.

He sent her a grateful smile. "I think I'll do that."

Stevie made a face over her shoulder at Daisy as she followed Mark out the door. "Spoilsport."

Moving to the window, Daisy watched them walk up the street. Stevie was laughing at something Mark said. Once again, she thanked her lucky stars that Phillip had suggested that they hire Mark six months ago.

Phillip.

Daisy sighed. The truth was, Phillip Baldwin was a good man. He was perfect for her, really. They put their obligations to their families and their work first. They would have a very happy life together.

Turning, Daisy began to pick up books that her lunchtime customers had left on the tables and chairs. In about half an hour, the store would be busy again with the after-work browsers. Quickly, she straightened a display of men's adventure fiction, then refilled the candy jar near a selection of romance novels.

As she glanced down at one of the books, she

tried to picture Phillip on the cover, holding her in his arms. The image just wouldn't form.

Daisy frowned. Maybe she and Phillip were *too* right for each other. Plus, they didn't have any obstacles standing in their way. In books, it was always the star-crossed lovers who seemed to have a better chance at falling in love. Like Romeo and Juliet.

And they ended up dead, she reminded herself.

But a person could die of boredom too.

Turning, she strode to the computer and sat down. She needed that magic bed.

Five minutes later, she hung up her phone. A very nice man with an Irish brogue had confirmed her reservation. One week from tonight, Daisy would find out if her decision made her a true romantic or just a plain, old ding-a-ling.

ONE WEEK LATER, Daisy strode purposefully along a crowded Manhattan sidewalk toward her Uncle Daniel's office building. Today was D day. She'd been preparing all week for it. She'd bought new clothes and gotten her hair lightened and cut in a new short style.

Tonight she and Phillip were going to sleep in that magic bed, fall in love with each other and live happily ever after.

Daisy shot a defiant glance at the darkening sky. She was not about to let the huge storm whipping its way up the Atlantic coast spoil it for her. The weatherman was predicting two feet of snow by midnight, with even higher accumulations in the Catskills. Small, steadily falling flakes stung her cheeks. Suddenly, Daisy slid, skidding along the sidewalk and nearly colliding with an oncoming pedestrian. Finding her balance, she glared at the thin film of snow already covering the streets.

She had to convince Phillip to leave the office right now. She had her car parked in a garage just three blocks away. They could beat the rush-hour traffic and be out of Manhattan in less than half an hour.

What if he says no?

Daisy's confidence wavered as she recalled Phillip's initial reaction when she'd proposed the weekend getaway. They'd actually had their first argument. Not that Phillip had raised his voice. He'd merely pointed out to her how impractical it would be for him to leave the office two weeks before their honeymoon. It would be much more prudent for him to work this weekend.

Her practical side had fully comprehended the logic of his argument.

It was her wild and romantic side that had prompted her to storm out of the room.

Of course, Phillip had come after her and apologized, laughing and teasing her about "bridal jitters." And he'd very nicely agreed to go with her. But when he'd given her a fond, indulgent kiss on the forehead, she'd had to stifle the almost uncontrollable impulse to run out of the room again.

What if he used the storm to get out of the whole thing?

What was she going to do then? Kidnap him and throw him in the trunk of her car?

As Daisy stepped into the revolving door and pushed against the glass, she looked at her reflection, hoping to shore up her confidence. The woman staring right back at her was the new Daisy Hanover. Gone was the ex-librarian bookstore owner who wore jeans and bulky sweaters and continually had to keep her glasses from falling off her face. In the old Daisy's place was a blonde, dressed for success, with wide green eyes...desperate green eyes.

It was the same old Daisy Hanover wearing a disguise and desperately trying to get her fiancé into a magic bed.

Desperate Daisy. As she stepped into the lobby and strode toward the elevators, she could picture the words spelled out in neon letters over her head. Blinking on and off.

And the clock was ticking. Tapping her foot, she watched the elevator doors slide open. Then she fought her way through the wave of people flowing out into the lobby.

"Two feet by midnight."

"Those weather reports are never right."

"Look, it's starting to accumulate already."

As the doors slid shut, Daisy reached to press the button. It was only as fingertips brushed against hers that she realized she wasn't alone in the elevator.

Though the touch was light, it made an impression. She was aware of hardness, strength. The hand was masculine, the fingers lean, elegant.

The contact only lasted for an instant, but it had been potent. She felt the heat spreading through her, and the sudden, almost shocking coolness as the stranger withdrew his hand.

Disturbed, curious, she took a quick look at her companion.

Dangerous was the first word that slipped into her mind. The silk shirt, the impeccably tailored jacket and crisply creased slacks did nothing to dispel her impression that the man beneath the clothes was someone who would acquit himself well in a fight.

James Bond was her second thought. With a slight frown, she studied the stranger more closely, trying to pin down what had triggered the association. The face in profile was certainly handsome enough to compete with the actors who had played Bond in the movies. She was sure that the lean, aristocratic features, the dark eyebrows and hair would be very photogenic. And then there was all that subdued elegance on the outside trying to disguise the predator within. But none of the movie Bonds had ever worn a mustache. Nor had they worn cowboy boots.

Cowboy boots? Daisy blinked and stared. They were hidden beneath neatly cuffed trousers, but they were definitely cowboy boots. More curious than ever, she glanced quickly back at the man's face and found herself staring into the bluest pair of eyes she'd ever seen. They were cool, seemingly bottomless. And she suddenly had the strangest sensation that she was sinking. Fast. Into very deep waters. But just before the waters closed over her head, what she felt was…kinship?

The next thing she knew, hard hands were gripping her, shaking her.

"Are you all right?"

The voice was smooth, deep. It was the slight trace of a British accent that had Daisy's eyes snapping open. The elevator had stopped, the doors were sliding open. And the man staring at her with a trace of annoyance in his eyes was a complete stranger. So why had she felt that curious sense of connection?

He gave her another little shake. "Are you all right?" he repeated.

Drawing in a deep breath, she managed to say, "I'm fine." At least she would be as soon as he stopped touching her. His hands were only gripping her arms to steady her, but she felt the response shoot through her as if their bodies were pressed together. Tightly.

Shaking her head to rid it of the image, she said, "It's just vertigo. I get an attack whenever I ride in an elevator."

"You're sure?" he asked as he guided her through the elevator doors.

"Absolutely," Daisy said, though it took a lot of willpower to remain upright when he dropped his hands to his sides. "This happens to me all the time. See." She lifted her arms and summoned a bright smile. "Wristbands. I wear them to combat the vertigo. They're going to kick in any minute."

Frowning, he studied her for a moment.

Keeping her smile in place, Daisy aimed her

gaze for his left ear. If she looked into those eyes again… She saw him nod briefly, then he finally turned and walked down the hall. Daisy took one quick step back toward the wall, leaned against it for support and let out the breath she'd been holding.

Good grief, she thought as she watched his long-legged stride carry him away. Did practically fainting into James Bond's arms make her one of the Bond girls?

Don't even start with that fantasizing, she lectured herself. *James Bond is a fictional character. He doesn't exist in real life. And you have a perfectly wonderful fiancé who does.*

Still, Daisy couldn't take her eyes off the stranger. Until he turned into the offices of Hanover Securities. Then she took two deep breaths and followed in his footsteps.

As Logan Campbell strode down the hallway, he fought the urge to glance back at the woman he'd just assisted off the elevator. She'd caught his attention the moment she'd spun out of the revolving door into the lobby almost as if she were a part of the storm the weatherman was predicting. In that one instant, he'd noticed everything about her—the slender body, the delicate features and the blond hair, mussed as if some man had just run his hands through it. His first impression that she was fragile enough to be blown into the lobby by a good wind had immediately been contradicted. In her pell-mell rush toward the elevators, she'd radiated speed, energy, purpose.

It was the contradiction that had kept his eyes on her. This was a woman who would create her own storms.

And then she'd turned the tables on him. As the doors of the elevator slid shut and the car shot upward, he'd felt her eyes on him. He'd wanted to blend in with any one of the hundreds of Wall Street brokers who might have an appointment with Phillip Baldwin today, so he'd chosen his disguise carefully, right down to the last detail. But he was sure that the woman standing next to him had been cataloging each one. Hell, she'd probably be able to pick him out of a lineup if she had to.

It was then that he'd thrown caution to the winds and turned to face her. For one second, as he'd looked into those emerald-green eyes, he'd had the oddest feeling that he'd met her before. But he hadn't. Logan Campbell tracked down missing persons for a living. He never forgot a face.

It was then that she'd suddenly swayed and he'd reached out to grab hold of her. Touching her had been a mistake, Logan thought as he reached the door to Hanover Securities. He'd been mistaken about knowing her, but not about his response when he'd held her. The swift burn of desire that had moved through him, tightening every muscle in his body, had been unmistakable. And that one second when his mind had completely emptied was unprecedented.

Even now, Logan was surprised at the amount of control it took not to look back at her one more time before he walked through the office door. As curious as he might be, he didn't have any time to waste on green-eyed witches.

What he needed was a vacation, Logan thought as he flashed a smile at the receptionist and headed down the corridor to find Phillip Baldwin's office. His assistant, Ray, had been bugging him for months to take some time off. Perhaps he would. First he had to clear up the little matter of Eddie Maplethorpe's death. And Phillip Baldwin was the client of record for that case. Though Campbell Investigations had handled other cases for Hanover Securities, he'd never met Baldwin before.

Spotting the name on a door, Logan entered without knocking and flashed another smile, this time at the large efficient-looking woman whose desk was stationed firmly between him and the door to Baldwin's office. The nameplate on the desk proclaimed Ms. Archer.

The woman, who had the face and demeanor of a drill sergeant, frowned up at him. "May I help you?"

"I want to see Mr. Baldwin," said Logan.

"He's busy right—"

Logan was walking through the door before the drill sergeant made it out of her chair. Closing it firmly in her face, he focused his full attention on the man behind the desk.

"Yes, may I help you?"

Crossing the room, Logan took time to study Phillip Baldwin. Medium height, short brown hair, hazel eyes. In spite of the slender build, Baldwin had the soft body of a man who spent hours behind a desk. He also had the careful, guarded eyes of a political animal—someone who would constantly filter and adjust his reactions for the benefit of an audience. By the time Logan reached the desk, the initial surprise he'd seen in the man's eyes had vanished.

Ignoring the hand Baldwin was extending, Logan said, "Early this morning, an attorney named Eddie Maplethorpe was killed by a hit-and-run driver."

"What? No, you must be mistaken... Who... who are you?"

The shock could have been feigned. But Logan doubted Baldwin was skilled enough to turn several shades paler at will. And the offered hand was trembling as Logan grasped it firmly in his. It was also damp.

"Logan Campbell from Campbell Investigations. I spoke with you on the phone last Friday when I agreed to locate Eddie Maplethorpe for you. You said a client wanted to talk to him about a will. I want to talk to that client."

"Oh, yes. Now I remember." Summoning up a smile, Phillip gestured to a nearby chair. "I should have recognized your voice. This is a shock. You say Mr. Maplethorpe was run down? Surely it was an accident—"

"Too much of a coincidence to my way of thinking," Logan said as he settled himself into a chair. "The man was a practicing attorney in Brooklyn for over twenty years. Then suddenly he disappears, without informing his associates or his landlady. I track him down at your request, and one day after I do, he's dead." Looking up, he met Baldwin's eyes directly. "I don't like the feeling that I may have fingered someone for a hit. Who asked you to find Maplethorpe?"

"Look, I..." Picking up a pen, Phillip began to draw it through his fingers. "Our clients demand confidentiality. I'm afraid I can't—"

"That confidentiality routine won't work with the police. But I haven't spoken with them yet. It might be less of a hassle if your client would agree to speak with me. Your choice."

Phillip's knuckles had turned white where he gripped the pen. Placing it carefully on the desk, he said, "I'll be frank with you. I'm in a very delicate position here. Let's suppose I promise you that in this case you don't have any cause for concern." He raised a hand to prevent Logan from interrupting. "The person involved here wouldn't have, couldn't have, had anything to do with Maplethorpe's death. She's not even a client. She's my fiancée, Daisy Hanover."

"The same Daisy Hanover who became two million dollars richer when Eddie Maplethorpe came forward with Angela Hanover's new will?" At Baldwin's surprised expression, Logan smiled. "I make it a habit to thoroughly investigate the cases I take on. Angela Hanover's will was the last case Maplethorpe handled before he disappeared. His landlady thought he was taking a vacation to celebrate. Why did your fiancée want him found?"

"She wanted to talk to him. She and her cousin each inherited two million. She's concerned about the way the younger girl is reacting to the money, and she wanted to reassure herself of her aunt's state of mind when she wrote the will."

As Phillip continued to talk about his fiancée and her concerns, Logan studied the man sitting across from him, measuring his explanation against the facts. A young woman wanted to locate the man who'd drawn up the will making her two million dollars richer just to make sure of her aunt's state of mind when she'd signed the will? It just didn't wash. And Logan couldn't fail to notice that Phillip Baldwin, though he was trying hard to conceal it, was a very nervous man.

And why would Maplethorpe have disappeared in the first place? Why wasn't he just sitting in his office waiting for Miss Daisy Hanover's phone call? And Logan was fully aware the man sitting across from him had a vested interest in the will. After all, he was engaged to marry the heiress.

Then again, maybe he was overreacting. It was just possible that Maplethorpe's death had been an accident.

"I'll have to talk to Miss Hanover." Logan caught the quick flicker of annoyance in Phillip's eyes before it was masked.

"I want to be present," Phillip said. "Her aunt's death has been very hard on her, and I don't want her upset. The earliest I can arrange it is Monday. She's out of town for the weekend."

The office door flew open, and the woman from the elevator blew into the room with Ms. Archer in hot pursuit.

"Phillip, I'm sorry to interrupt," she began as Phillip moved quickly to take her arm.

"I'm in the middle of something," Phillip said. He was frowning as he urged her toward the door.

"I tried to stop her," put in the drill sergeant.

"It's all right, Ms. Archer." Turning back to Logan, Phillip said, "If you'll excuse me for a minute, Campbell?" At Logan's nod, he quickly ushered the two women out of the room and shut the door behind him.

Rising, Logan's first impulse was to move to the door and open it a crack so he could get another look at the green-eyed witch from the elevator. Annoyed with himself, he walked toward the window and tried to concentrate on the problem at hand. Why wasn't he satisfied with the explanation Baldwin had given him?

Because of the will, he decided. Why would a woman of Angela Hanover's background use a third-rate lawyer from Brooklyn to draw up a will? Obviously, she wanted to keep it a secret from her husband. But the chances of her running into or being referred to Eddie Maplethorpe were slim to none. From what Logan had been able to find out, she'd been ill and hadn't left her husband's Westchester estate for years.

Turning, Logan's glance fell on a framed photograph sitting on the desk. He recognized the tall man with the receding hairline immediately. Daniel Hanover had come from money. His father had built up his own successful business. Then he and his son Daniel had spent their lives amassing even more wealth. Their small family-owned investment firm was one of the most successful on Wall Street for its size. The fragile-looking woman next to him in the photo must be his wife, Angela. And sitting in front, the two children. No, not two, Logan corrected himself. The oldest girl was a niece, the daughter of the black sheep of the family. But Angela Hanover had evidently thought of her as a daughter, because she'd left Daisy half of her estate.

Lifting the picture, Logan studied it more carefully. Daisy Hanover had honey-blond hair that was struggling to escape from the knot on the top of her head. And glasses that had settled halfway down her nose. And...Logan's eyes suddenly narrowed...take away those glasses, lighten the hair, shorten it, and she'd be a dead ringer for the woman he'd met in the elevator.

Was that why Baldwin had escorted her from the room so quickly? He'd said she wouldn't be available until Monday. Moving to the door, Logan eased it open a crack.

She and Baldwin were standing at the outer door to his office. Even from a distance, Logan could feel the tension between them.

"I want to wait here for you," she was saying. "Haven't you understood one thing I've—"

"What I understand is that you're upset." The hushed urgency in Phillip's voice contrasted with the smile on his face. "Something has come up, and I can't leave right now."

"But later will be too late. The snow—"

"Be reasonable," Phillip said as he urged her out into the hallway. "I don't want to rush up there just to get snowed in at that cabin. I never understood why you wanted to go to that place anyway. It's not at all like my sweet, practical Daisy."

"That's the whole—"

"Shh." Drawing her close, Phillip pressed a kiss against her forehead. "We don't want to create a scene in front of Ms. Archer, do we? Now, I want you to be a good girl and go home. I don't want you to have trouble getting back to your uncle's house. I'll call you—"

"Mr. Baldwin," Ms. Archer said. "Mr. Hanover is on the line."

When Phillip turned to take the call, Logan had a clear view of the kaleidoscope of emotions flickering across Daisy's face. Disappointment, anger...longing? Even from a distance of ten feet, he could see the glint of tears in her eyes, and he could feel the passion. Hot, vibrant, it had pulled that instant response from him in the elevator, and it was reaching out to him now. As her eyes shifted and met his, he once more felt the pull. He wanted...he needed...

And then Phillip was swearing softly under his breath as he hung up the phone and turned back to Daisy. "I told you to go."

"All right." Moving toward him, she took a folded piece of paper out of her pocket. "But I'm not going home. I'm going to drive up to the cabin. These are the directions." She slammed the paper down on the desk. "If you change your mind, you'll find me there." Daisy Hanover whirled around and left the office with Phillip Baldwin hot on her heels.

"Wait. Daisy, you're overreacting..."

Logan waited until Baldwin's voice faded. One thing was clear. The man didn't want him to talk to Daisy Hanover. But he intended to do just that. Opening the door, he slipped into the outer office.

Ms. Archer glanced up and shot a glare at him.

"It looks as though Mr. Baldwin might be a while," Logan said. "He mentioned coffee…"

For a brief moment, the drill sergeant hesitated. Then she rose. "Certainly. Cream and sugar?"

The moment she reached the cabinet and turned to lift the coffeepot, Logan pocketed the brochure Daisy Hanover had left.

"On second thought, why don't you tell Mr. Baldwin that I'll get back to him at a more convenient time?"

Logan felt the heat of Ms. Archer's glare as he stepped into the hall.

2

ONCE THE REVOLVING doors spun her out onto the street, Daisy skidded to a dead stop. She had to figure out what to do. Her brain hadn't kicked in once during that long ride down in the elevator. It had been numb. She'd been numb. Paralyzed by the emotions that had washed over her in Phillip's office.

The disappointment she could understand. She'd been depending on this weekend to solve her problem. And the anger was natural too. It wasn't just that Phillip had refused to leave early. He'd refused to go at all. And he'd promised.

"Is it his fault that you don't have the power to persuade him?"

As if in agreement with the little voice in her head, a gust of wind blew an icy spray of snow and a pedestrian into her.

"Sorry," murmured the man as he caught his balance and moved around her.

Daisy felt the quick prick of tears again behind her eyelids. The truth hurt. And for a moment up there in Phillip's office, her disappointment had tilted into despair.

That's when she'd suddenly become aware of the man standing in the shadows behind the door to Phillip's office. Her elevator man, James Bond. She couldn't see him as much as sense him. And she'd felt again that strange sense of kinship.

It was because of him that she'd found the courage to make an end run around Ms. Archer's desk and burst into Phillip's office. All she'd had to do was remember the way James always charmed his way past Miss Moneypenny into M's office.

But she hadn't managed to charm Phillip into anything. He'd told her as he'd put her on the elevator that she was acting like a child, that he was sure she'd think better of his decision when she'd come to her senses. That it was madness to think of racing off to the Catskills in a storm. And that she'd always known that he had to put business before anything else.

It had been such a relief when the elevator doors had silenced his droning voice.

But what on earth was she going to do now? Be a "good girl" and go home?

Suddenly she thought of her elevator man again. She couldn't imagine one of James Bond's girls simply going home. They were never good girls. Of course, James had always found a way to fit them into his crowded schedule.

Lifting her chin, Daisy turned on her heel and strode down the sidewalk. She was going to that cabin in the Catskills by herself.

Would Phillip worry about her and come after her?

And then the thought struck her. Would the

bed still work if only one of the parties slept in it?

"That bed will work on the same day that pigs fly!" said the practical voice in her head.

The other little voice held its peace as Daisy battled the wind and snow to reach her car.

"I'M PUTTING my money on the heiress." Raynaldo Juarez tapped his finger on the screen of his computer. "Baldwin looks squeaky-clean to me."

Logan turned from the window in his office to study his assistant. "You haven't met him."

"I haven't met the heiress either. Is she pretty?"

Ignoring the question, Logan said, "What exactly did you turn up on Baldwin?"

"He has an MBA from Harvard, he worked for two Wall Street investment firms before he was recruited by Daniel Hanover himself."

"All that means is that he isn't some con man off the street. He could still be crooked. Dig deeper. And keep him under surveillance."

Ray smiled. "And in the meantime, I suppose you'll be personally investigating the heiress?"

Logan glanced at his watch, then out the window of his office. Daisy Hanover had more than an hour's head start on him. And the snow was falling more heavily with each passing minute.

When he left the Hanover building, he'd followed her to her garage, then hailed a cab and tailed her until he realized that she was indeed headed for the Catskills. At that point he'd gone back to his office to make some arrangements with Ray.

"Why are you so sure it's Miss Hanover?" he asked.

"Because she's the niece, not the daughter, yet she gets half the money. If you're right and the will Maplethorpe produced is a fake, I'm betting she had a hand in drawing it up."

Shoving his hands in his pockets, Logan continued to stare out the window. What Ray said made sense. And he didn't have one good reason to disagree. Except for a pair of green eyes that had bewitched him.

A sudden gust of wind blew icy pellets against the windowpane.

"I need to borrow your car," Logan said.

Ray dug out his keys. "I knew it. You're going to follow her to that cabin."

"If she made it. And make sure you keep me informed about Baldwin. If he changes his mind and decides to join us, give me some warning." Grabbing the keys from Ray, he headed for the door.

"Right, boss. Drive safely."

DAISY BREATHED a sigh of relief as she made out the dark shape of the cabin through a heavy curtain of falling snow. It resembled a small, squat box with a covered porch and a lean-to at the side. A light in the window winked a welcome. To Daisy, it looked like heaven. Keeping her foot steady on the gas pedal, she inched her car toward the lean-to.

More than once, she'd begun to wonder if she

would really make it. Especially after dark had fallen with the suddenness of a lid clapping onto a pot. She didn't want to think about where she might have ended up if the map hadn't been so accurate or if the visibility hadn't suddenly cleared each time she had to take a turn.

Here at last, she thought as she opened the car door and wiggled out. She heard it then—music? It reminded her of an old-fashioned music box or... She glanced around. The wind was still blowing furiously, slapping snow against the roof of the lean-to. But she couldn't spot any wind chimes.

With a shrug, she ignored her cramped legs, pulled her bag out of the back seat and hurried up the cabin steps onto the porch. The key to the front door was under the mat just as the man on the phone had said. And a light over the mantel was lit to welcome her.

Shutting the door quickly behind her, Daisy let her gaze sweep the place, taking in the wood-planked floor, faded rugs and chintz sofa. The room was small and entirely dominated by the fireplace that filled one wall. Moving quickly toward it, she lit the fire that had already been laid. Moments later, flames began to lick hungrily at the wood, shooting sparks up the chimney and spreading warmth into the room.

She was on her way to the kitchen to explore, when she noticed the note on the coffee table. The message was brief.

Enjoy your stay. If you care to remain beyond the weekend, the cabin is yours. The refrigerator is stocked for a week, and I won't be back to clean until next Friday.

The caretaker, a man with a lovely Irish brogue, had told her as much on the phone when she'd made the reservation for the weekend. He'd assured her that it was the same price for a longer stay, and that most guests chose to linger. As Daisy glanced around the room again, she couldn't help wondering if she would have been able to persuade Phillip to extend their visit.

Fat chance. She hadn't even been able to convince him to come up here at all.

She glanced down at the key she still held in her hand, then set it on the table. She wasn't going to lock the door. Maybe Phillip would change his mind and join her.

It was then that she heard the music again. Not wind chimes, she thought. Try as she might, she couldn't recognize the instrument. Faint but clear, it seemed to be coming from the bedroom. Following the sound, she pushed open the door, turned on the light and forgot completely about the music.

The bed filled the room. Four intricately carved posts nearly brushed the ceiling. Reaching out, she touched one. The richly hued wood was satiny smooth, and it certainly looked old. Her research into Celtic myths had revealed that oak was a sacred wood. Moving closer, she saw the interlocking circles carved into the headboard. Above them was the inscription. The language certainly looked ancient.

Just seeing the bed made the claims on the Web site more believable somehow. Stitched into the coverlet thrown across the bed were the same interlocking circles carved on the head-board. They looked like wedding rings. Moving closer, she ran her hand over the rings.

Immediately, an image slipped into her mind. She and Phillip lying on that white coverlet, limbs intertwined.

Except… Daisy jerked her hand off the bed as if it had burned her. For a moment, it hadn't been Phillip she imagined rolling around on that bed with. It had been her elevator man. James Bond. For an instant, she'd felt the press of those hard hands on her just as she had in the elevator. Heat arrowed through her.

Slowly, carefully, as if she were about to touch a hot wire, she put her hand on the bed again. The image didn't return.

Daisy frowned. Did she want it to? She couldn't recall ever fantasizing so clearly about a man before. Especially about one who was a complete stranger.

Shaking her head, she focused her attention back on the huge bed. If it had been made by the ancient Celts, it almost certainly had to have been transported in some kind of magical way to the New World, Daisy decided. Running her hand along the footboard, Daisy moved to the other side. And then she saw it. A footstool. That would solve the problem of how she was going to climb into it.

So that she could sleep alone.

For the third time that day, Daisy felt the prick

of tears in her eyes. Was that partly why she'd agreed to marry Phillip? Because she was lonely?

Was she lonely enough to settle for a man she didn't love and who didn't love her, a man who made love to her as if she were just another appointment he needed to check off on his calendar?

Ignoring the little band of pain that had tightened around her heart, Daisy turned and started for the other room. She made it to the doorway before she recalled the music she'd heard earlier. Turning, she let her gaze sweep the room, but there weren't any speakers. And no sign of wires. In fact, there was nothing in the room at all except the bed. Where was the sound coming from? she wondered.

Well, she had all weekend to solve the mystery. Right now, she was going to have a hot bath.

LOGAN SWORE SOFTLY under his breath as he downshifted into second gear and pressed his foot harder on the gas pedal. He felt rather than saw that the road had begun to climb again. During the past hour, the falling snow had grown thicker, heavier. Each time the windshield wipers struggled back and forth, they seemed to push away bigger and bigger clumps of snow.

What he was driving through right now was one continuous whiteout. He would have missed the turn off the main highway a ways back if the visibility hadn't almost miraculously cleared for a few moments.

As he felt the Jeep begin to slow, he gave it more gas. It was crucial to keep moving. If he lost the forward momentum, he might not ever make it to the top of the hill.

Eyes burning, he peered through the windshield and saw nothing. For the hundredth time, he wished that he could have gotten an earlier start.

His progress had been hampered by the tangle of traffic leaving the city and now by the steady accumulation of snow. But if his calculations were correct, Miss Hanover should have been at the cabin before the worst of the storm hit. So far none of the abandoned vehicles he'd passed along the road had been hers.

His fingers dug into the wheel as he felt the tires begin to spin frantically. He counted ten long seconds, and each one of them twisted the knot of tension at the back of his neck. He hadn't dared to stop since he'd turned off the main highway, but he could tell that the snow must reach halfway up the Jeep's tires by now. If he could just reach the top of the hill, the quarter mile beyond it would be easier. And then he'd be at the last turnoff. He could walk the last two miles from there. Just then the tires caught and began to chew snow again. Logan's hand tightened on the wheel to hold the Jeep steady.

He thought about the place Daisy Hanover had gone. "A romantic and secluded cabin." That's the way the brochure had described the it.

Well, he wasn't looking for romance. He'd

stopped believing in it that night years ago when his brother had betrayed him.

Logan frowned. Now, why had that thought popped into his mind? He was following Daisy Hanover through a blinding snowstorm because he wanted some answers. Was she really the innocent-looking, practical girl she'd appeared to be in the family photo? Or was she involved in a plot to steal money from the family that had raised her since she was a two-year-old? Once he had the answers to his questions, he would have no further interest in Daisy Hanover.

There was no denying that the woman in the elevator had been a sharp right turn away from the girl in the family photo. And to head into the Catskills during a blizzard smacked of pure recklessness. And passion...the hot, vibrant kind he'd sensed simmering in her when he'd held her in the elevator, and when she'd appeared in Baldwin's office. He hadn't even been touching her then. But he'd wanted to. For a moment, he'd wanted more than anything to set that passion free, to see where it would lead....

The Jeep's engine growled, and the tires once more spun out of traction. Swearing under his breath again, Logan reined in his wandering thoughts and concentrated on driving.

"C'mon," he crooned. "C'mon." Finally the tires caught, and Logan had to fight to keep the car from swerving to the right. Then suddenly, he felt it. The road was leveling again. Squinting, he tried to see through the white wall the headlights couldn't pierce. As the Jeep inched along, he risked a quick look at the odometer whenever he could. It was his only hope of finding that turnoff. A little over two-tenths of a mile to go. Leaning closer to the windshield, Logan kept his foot steady on the gas pedal.

Even with the odometer's help, he might have missed it. But once again, the visibility cleared, just enough for him to spot the two stone posts. They were almost completely buried in snow. Abandoning the Jeep, Logan pulled the hood of his jacket up and struck out down the almost invisible road. According to the map, the cabin was two miles away.

The walk wasn't easy, but Logan found that the exercise gradually eased the tension from his body. More than once he would have wandered off the road if he hadn't been able to catch a glimpse now and then of indentations in the snow from tire tracks of a single car. At times, he could have sworn he heard something other than the wind blowing so furiously. Some kind of music.

He wasn't sure if it was an instrument or a chant. During the last mile, the sound tantalized him, growing louder at times, leading him to believe that the cabin would lie just beyond the next bend in the road. Then suddenly, there it was. A change in the wind cleared the snow so that he could see the squat little box set in a cluster of trees. Logan moved toward it.

He was on the porch when the door blew open. Hadn't she locked it? The moment he was inside, he shut the door and threw the latch. At the same moment, a bone-weary tiredness settled on him. He drew in a deep breath and let it out. Though the room was very dim, lit only by the light from a dying fire, it appeared to be empty. Evidently, Miss Hanover had retired for the night. Through one door he glimpsed a kitchen. Through another, a bed.

Logan headed for the fireplace, took off his boots and set them near the hearth. He tried the light on the mantel, but it didn't work. A power failure explained the chill in the room. He laid more logs on the embers. Once the flames began to lick hungrily at the wood, he turned.

It was then that he saw her. Daisy Hanover lay fast asleep on the couch, totally cocooned in a white coverlet and looking as innocent as an angel. Her short hair was spread out on the pillow, framing her face like a halo. He could see separate strands of honey and gold. Without even being aware of it, he moved toward her. His hand was inches away from her hair, when he snatched it back.

If he touched her now, he wouldn't stop.

The realization stunned him.

Logan studied Daisy's face. He'd been fooled by the illusion of innocence before, he reminded himself. And it had led to betrayal. No one was really what they appeared to be. Hadn't he learned that lesson from Lucy Farnsworth?

And hadn't he come here to find out who this woman was and what she knew about Eddie Maplethorpe's death?

Still, he was reluctant to wake her. And he was exhausted too. It would be better to wait until morning.

He thought briefly of carrying her into the bed

and taking her place on the couch. But she would be warmer near the fire.

And he was better off not touching her at all. It was then that he heard the music again. The same haunting sound that had beckoned him to the cabin. It seemed to be coming from the bedroom, but as he moved closer, it didn't grow any louder. Was he imagining it?

No. Logan shook his head. It was a trick of the wind, not of his mind. He was tired. The drive and the walk through the woods had only added to the exhaustion that he'd been feeling for some time now. What he desperately needed was to sleep.

He made his way to the bedroom and bumped immediately into a bed. Feeling his way along the side, he stripped out of his clothes, set his gun on the nightstand and slipped under the covers. In the morning, he would deal with Daisy Hanover. He would have his answers, and he'd be on his way.

DAISY WOKE SLOWLY as if she were gradually floating to the surface from somewhere deep underwater. She heard music. The kind that mythical mermaids might play to lure sailors closer and closer. Lovely and soothing, it pulled at her. She opened her eyes briefly, then closed them. It was still dark. Holding herself still, she willed herself to sink once more beneath the surface. To fall once more into her dream.

It had seemed so real. She'd been in his arms, pressed close. His body had been harder and even more unyielding than she'd imagined.

And his mouth. It had been close, so close she could feel the warmth of his breath against her lips. In a moment she would taste him. She'd felt the pressure of his thumb beneath her chin raising it, and she'd lifted her gaze past his lips to his eyes. Even as his mouth closed over hers, she'd known it wasn't Phillip she was kissing. Phillip's eyes weren't blue.

Using all of her willpower, Daisy snapped her own eyes open again. This time she didn't close them. Those blue eyes belonged to the man in the elevator.

She made herself take slow steady breaths. It had only been a dream. There was absolutely no reason for the quick sprint of panic that moved through her.

Or was it anticipation?

Pushing the traitorous thought away, Daisy concentrated on details—the chill in the air, the softness of the sofa cushions beneath her, the scratch of the wool coverlet against her skin. And the music. It was fainter now. But she was going to have to find out where it was coming from. Focusing on details was a trick her Aunt Angela had taught her when Daisy was a little girl, and it had always kept her nightmares at bay.

Except this hadn't been a nightmare, really. The man in the elevator had slipped into her thoughts quite frequently during the day. It was probably only natural that he would make an appearance in her dreams. She wasn't going to put any Freudian interpretation on it. And she wouldn't even be dreaming of her fictional

James Bond if she'd been able to persuade Phillip to come with her.

Outside, she heard the wind whistle sharply, whipping against the cabin walls and rattling the panes of glass. The scent of burnt wood grew suddenly stronger. The fire was dead, but... She turned to look at the lamp on the table next to her. She could have sworn she'd left it on. Reaching for the switch, she turned it with no result.

First a blizzard, now a power failure. And she'd come to the Catskills for romance.

No, she thought with sudden clarity. She'd come here to find true love.

And if there was any chance at all that the bed in the other room had magical powers, she'd better get into it.

She pulled the coverlet around her and stood up. Then, curling her toes against the cold floor, she made her way to the bedroom. Keeping her hands out in front of her, she felt for the footboard and let it guide her to the stool on the far side. A yawn overtook her as she climbed up and slipped beneath the covers.

The bed was warm, almost as if someone had been keeping it that way for her. She yawned for a second time as she snuggled into the pillows. Maybe she'd be a good girl and dream of Phillip.

Then again, maybe she'd be a Bond girl and dream of James.

LOGAN WAS TRAPPED in a dream—in that state somewhere between waking and sleeping. He could barely hear the music. It seemed to flow through him, soft as a whisper. He was with her. He could feel her heat. And her scent was seducing him. Since that first moment in the elevator, he hadn't been able to rid his mind of it. And now it had wrapped itself around him until he could no longer breathe without drawing it in.

When he reached out his hand and touched her, it was the most natural thing in the world to slip his arm beneath her and draw her closer until she was pressed fully against him, her breath warm near his ear. When she sighed, desire moved through him in a warm stream before he felt its tug. It was nothing like the hot, sharp twisting in his gut that he'd experienced before. Just a steadily growing pull.

He took his hand on a leisurely journey along the delicate line of her throat. He'd wanted to touch her from the moment his hand had brushed against hers. At last he could explore the soft curve of her breast, narrowness of her waist, and the smooth length of her thigh. Slowly, he repeated the journey, savoring the contrast between cool silk and warm skin.

He felt his need grow, but he didn't rush. He couldn't. His arm felt weighted, paralyzed almost, the way it often felt in a dream. He ran his fingers along the line of her jaw, felt the race of her pulse at her throat. The skin there was even softer than he'd imagined. The tug in his center grew stronger.

He'd never been a patient lover. But he couldn't seem to help himself. With her, he was learning that just the sound of a sigh could light a fire in his blood. The simple flutter of a pulse beneath his thumb could make that fire spread in a slow burn.

When he could no longer resist, no longer control his hunger, he used his thumb to tilt her chin upward, then brushed his lips against hers, teasing, tasting, then teasing again. Even when the blood began to pound in his head, urging him to hurry, he took his time, using his tongue to trace her lips so that he would never forget their shape. They were so soft, so moist. When they parted, when her breath shuddered into him, filling him, he finally pressed his mouth fully against hers.

She was back in her dream, Daisy thought as she poured herself into the kiss. She could hear the music she'd heard before, swirling around and flowing through her. But the body pressed against hers seemed so real. She'd been longing to kiss him, aching to feel the press of his lips against hers. She'd tried to imagine what it would be like. But she hadn't come close.

His mouth was so soft. Much softer than she'd imagined. And the flavor was intoxicating. Something dark and forbidden. She dipped her tongue in search of more, and a thick liquefying pleasure seeped through her. She'd never before dreamed anything like this. The body pressed against hers was so hard; the desire curling in her center was so strong. She didn't want to open her eyes and look. She didn't want him to disappear.

What she wanted, more than anything, was for him to go on kissing her in this slow, deliberate way, as if he had all the time in the world and intended to take it. There was such hunger here. She could feel it in the nip of his teeth on her lower lip. In the press of his hand at the back of her neck. Her own hunger sprang up to match it.

Threading her fingers into his hair, she shifted herself on top of him. As the music in her mind grew stronger, she pressed herself closer, arching against him in invitation. Once again, he began to touch her. Lean and firm, his hands moved over her thoroughly as if they were determined to memorize every inch of her—the firmness of her breast, the curve of her hip, the softness of her inner thigh. When his fingers lingered there, massaging, she felt her muscles melt.

Arching against him again, she urged him on. She wanted him to know every part of her, to remember her, to want her always. How could she have known that a man's hands could bring such pleasure? When his fingers found her and slipped into her, the sensations streamed through her. As he drove her higher and higher, he could have asked anything of her. And when he did, she felt herself explode into a thousand little pieces.

He held her close against him, absorbing each tremor, until her heartbeat slowed, and her breathing steadied. Then he whispered close to her ear, "Touch me."

She wasn't sure he'd said the words, but she'd heard them. Just as she heard the music singing in her veins as she ran her hands over him. She wanted them to memorize him, just as his hands had memorized her. She ran her fingers over his eyebrows, along his cheeks to the firm line of his jaw. His face was so strong. She would recognize him anywhere.

And his mouth. She had to taste him again. With her tongue, she traced his lips, drawing the pleasure out, letting the ache build again. She moved her mouth lower. The skin was damp at his throat, the taste addictive. And then drawing back, she had to touch him again, with more urgency this time, sliding her hands over him, pressing, possessing.

He wanted her. She could feel it in the way his muscles bunched beneath her palms, in the way his breath caught in his throat, then shuddered out. A dream couldn't possibly be this real. Could it? But reality had never brought this depth of pleasure. All she could be sure of was that she would remember this always.

Each separate sensation. The way his body trembled beneath hers. The race of his heart against her mouth. The hard press of his hands as he gripped her hips, shifted her beneath him.

For just a moment, she opened her eyes and watched him rise above her. She saw herself trapped in the depths of those blue eyes. And she knew he was everything she'd ever wanted.

When he slipped into her, it was still like a dream. But the music moved through him in a faster rhythm now. His moan merged with hers. Mouth to mouth, flesh to flesh, they began to move as one. He was only aware of her softness, her strength. Her. He could hear the sound of her breathing at his ear growing faster. He knew that they were reaching the end of their journey. For a moment, he fought against the speed, trying to hold back, wanting the pleasure to go on. In that moment his mind struggled too, trying to separate dream from reality. But it was too late.

He felt her tighten convulsively around him, felt the shudders of pleasure shoot through her. Digging his fingers into her hips, he pushed one more time, hard, and lost himself in her.

3

DAISY DREAMED she was lying on a huge old bed. She felt warm and cared for just as she had as a child when her aunt would hold her and rock her to sleep. Except it wasn't her aunt's arms that she was wrapped in. It was her lover's.

Lover's?

The word flitted around the edges of her subconscious like a worrisome gnat. In spite of all her efforts to the contrary, that one word finally penetrated her dream.

She was definitely in a bed. She could feel the smoothness of the sheets beneath her, the warmth of the covers above.

And there was definitely an arm around her.

Suddenly, as if a dam had opened, memories poured into her mind—the magic bed on the Web site, the scene in Phillip's office, her race against the blizzard.

The last thing she remembered was falling asleep on the couch and dreaming of her elevator man. Then the music had awakened her and she'd decided to give the bed a try.

She must have tumbled back into her dream. Except it had seemed so real. She couldn't possibly have conjured up a real lover. Could she? As soon as she pinched herself, she'd...

"Hmmmrrrm," growled a deep voice in her ear.

Daisy's eyes snapped open. The arm she'd pinched wasn't hers! And it didn't belong to any dream lover either. The body pressed against her back was very hard, very male, very real!

Who? Even as Daisy summoned up the courage to turn around, she knew who it would be.

"You!" They spoke the word together. And they sat up together, too. Just like a Greek chorus announcing a disaster, Daisy thought giddily as she stared into his blue eyes.

James Bond. It was her elevator man! He'd been on her mind, in her dreams. But the hand that still gripped her waist...it was real, *he* was real. And everything that had happened in her dream had been real!

Slipping from his embrace, she squirmed to the edge of the bed and dropped to the floor. She landed hard, pushing herself up with her hands.

"Are you all right?" he asked.

"Fine." Except for the fact she was naked. Daisy grabbed the edge of the quilt and pulled. It didn't give. She tried the coverlet next. It stuck to the bed like glue.

"Looking for this?"

She snatched the scrap of silk dangling from his fingers and hugged it to her breasts. She was very much aware that it didn't cover much. It would cover even less if she turned and raced for the door.

And where would she run to in the middle of

a blizzard? What in the world would a Bond girl do in a situation like this?

Get back in bed with him, dummy.

"You shaved your mustache."

He just grinned at her.

Marshaling every scrap of dignity she had, Daisy began to back away from the bed. Sometimes retreat was the only practical solution. "Well...I'll use the bathroom first if you don't mind."

"Fine," he said.

"Fine." She felt for the doorknob and gave it a twist. "I always think more clearly after a shower." Still walking backward, she made it into the bathroom and shut the door.

For a moment after Daisy disappeared, Logan didn't move. Oh, he wanted to all right. He wanted to follow her right into that bathroom and make love to her again, quickly, before either one of them had a chance to think. An image filled his mind of lifting her to the edge of the sink, wrapping her legs around him, and losing himself in her again. It was the intensity of the ache moving through him that stopped him.

What in the world was happening to him? Was he crazy?

It was the damn bed, he decided. He could still feel her warmth, smell her scent. Hell, he could still taste her. Throwing back the quilt, Logan dropped to the floor and scooped up his jeans.

What had happened to him was pretty clear. It hadn't been a dream. He'd actually made love to Daisy Hanover. Unable to stop himself, Logan glanced back at the bed.

A fantasy, that's what it had seemed like. All of his fantasies rolled into one. For a moment he could feel exactly what it had been like to hold her, to run his hands over her, then draw her closer. As the sensations poured through him, he heard the music again, the faint but unmistakable sound of...what?

Quickly, he glanced around the room, looking for a speaker, a wire, all the time trying to identify the instrument. It sounded like some kind of pipe the Greek god Pan would play. Or a song a siren might sing. Then suddenly it was gone. All he could hear was the sound of the shower running.

Giving his head a quick shake to clear it, Logan focused his attention on pulling on his clothes and securing his gun beneath the waistband of his jeans. What had happened during the night was no dream. He'd just slept with a suspect in a possible murder. Worse than that, he'd made love to a woman who was engaged to someone else.

Logan Campbell didn't poach.

Pulling his sweater over his head, Logan started to walk out of the room. Then he stopped short. For just a moment the walls of the cabin faded, and he was eighteen years old again, back in that motel room with Lucy Farnsworth. In the doorway stood his brother and Lucy's father, the Colonel. The Colonel was carrying a whip. Frowning, Logan shook his head again, to rid it of the image.

It had been years since he'd thought of the night his brother had accused him of sleeping with his betrothed. The night when Lucy Farnsworth had accused him of raping her. Yet in the short time since he'd first met Daisy, he'd thought of Lucy twice. Logan glanced at the bathroom door.

Why? Was it because after all these years, he still felt guilty about wanting a woman who belonged to someone else? He'd done more than want Lucy. He'd slept with her. He'd slept with his brother's fiancée.

At least Daisy Hanover hadn't accused him of rape.

And she'd been the one to join him in the bed. Yet, Logan would have bet his P.I. license that she hadn't done so with the idea of seducing him. She'd seemed as surprised at what had happened between them as he was. Frightened too. Those wide eyes of hers had reminded him of a baby deer he'd once caught in the sights of his rifle. Innocent. And scared to death.

For a moment, just before she'd wiggled away from him, he'd had an almost overwhelming urge to take her in his arms and just hold her.

And that would have been a big mistake.

Scowling, Logan walked out of the bedroom. He'd come here to get answers from Daisy Hanover, not to sleep with her or to protect her.

And he hadn't protected her. As the realization hit him, he stopped short and whirled back to stare into the bedroom. He'd never before made love to a woman without taking some kind of precautions. What had she done to him?

Enchanted him? Swearing under his breath, he turned and strode to the window. What he saw outside told him he'd have plenty of time for interrogating his suspect. Though the snow had stopped falling, the wind had removed any trace of his footsteps from the night before, and drifts covered the porch railing.

Moving to the fireplace, Logan noticed the lamp on the mantel was on. At least the power had been restored. Pulling on his boots, he started a fire. As soon as she was done with her shower, he and Ms. Hanover were going to have a long talk.

DAISY STARED at herself in the bathroom mirror. The water had been ice-cold. Her lips were blue. Her teeth were chattering. And she didn't have a clue about what to do with James Bond.

No, his name wasn't James Bond. The eyes of the woman in the mirror widened suddenly in shock. The truth was, she didn't know his name.

She'd just made love to a perfect stranger!

Dumb! She could picture the neon letters assembling themselves over her head.

At least the Bond girls *knew* who it was they were sleeping with.

Shivering, Daisy tightened the towel around her. What she needed was a plan. She hadn't come up with one in the shower. It wasn't possible to think straight when hypothermia was seconds away.

She'd just have to make something up as she went along.

Reaching for the doorknob, she prayed that

Mr. What's-his-name wouldn't still be in that bed. She didn't want to face him again until she was fully dressed.

Slowly, she open the door an inch and peeked. He wasn't there. Relief poured through her. Surely it was relief and not disappointment. Snatching her bag, she dug out socks, jeans and a sweater. But even after she'd dragged them on, she was still shivering. She grabbed the coverlet from the bed, wrapped herself in it and hurried out of the room before she lost her courage.

She found him in the kitchen, his hip braced against a counter, sipping coffee as he stared out the window. He looked bigger than he had in the elevator. Rougher too. His dark hair was mussed, his flannel shirt hung open, and the jeans fit snugly all the way down to his boots. He reminded her of a cowboy; not a cowpuncher on a ranch, but a gunslinger who rode from town to town righting wrongs.

Great, she told herself. What good was it going to do to stop fantasizing about James Bond if she was just going to switch to Shane?

Taking a deep breath, Daisy cleared her throat. The moment he turned, she poked her hand out of the coverlet. "I'm Daisy Hanover."

"Logan Campbell." Moving toward her, he grasped her hand firmly, then frowned. "You're freezing." Taking her arm, he urged her into the living room, settled her on the couch and tucked the coverlet around her. When he had the fire blazing, he turned to study her. With her hair damp and pulled back from her face, she looked young, defenseless. Her skin had the pale translucence of fine porcelain, ready to shatter. "Coffee?"

At her nod, he strode to the kitchen, filled two mugs and carried them back to the fire. "We have to talk," he said, sitting down on the coffee table and facing her.

She reached for her coffee and gripped it in both hands.

After a moment, Logan said, "You're supposed to drink it."

Daisy took a long swallow, then still holding the mug tightly, she raised her eyes to meet his. "I'm not sure what to say. I've never before had to introduce myself to someone after...I mean... What do we do next? Exchange driver's licenses?"

It was Logan's turn to clear his throat. "No, we talk about protection. I didn't use anything."

"Oh. I didn't even think..." She took a deep breath, then let it out again. "But I'm on the Pill. I'm getting married in two—*Phillip!*"

Logan rescued her mug and set it on the table.

Daisy stared at him in horror. "I just remembered Phillip... I haven't thought about him even once since we...since... What's the matter with me? What am I thinking...?" Daisy let the sentence trail off as she realized exactly what she was thinking of. The same thing she'd been thinking of since she woke up. A cold shower hadn't helped. And looking into Logan Campbell's eyes didn't help either. They were hypnotizing her, pulling her under, just as they had from that first moment on the elevator.

It was a mistake to have gotten this close to

him, their knees touching. She felt breathless, weak, as if she'd run a very long race up a steep hill. She dropped her gaze to his mouth, then realized that was a mistake too. One look was enough to bring the memories flooding back—the heat, his taste. She could hear the music she'd heard in the night, soft as the movement of a breeze over the strings of a harp. And she felt pulled toward him. She wanted...she needed...

"No!" The word sounded breathless to Daisy's ears, but it was enough to make both of them draw back. She took a deep breath and tried again. "You've got to understand. I'm engaged to Phillip Baldwin. He was the one who was supposed to be in that bed. I'm not sure how to explain..."

"You don't owe me an explanation," Logan said, watching her intently.

"Well, maybe I'd like to be able to explain it to myself. I'll certainly have to explain it to Phillip. We're going to be married. He was the one who was supposed to be in that bed with me."

"Are you saying that you thought it was Phillip you were making love with last night?" Logan asked.

Daisy closed her eyes, then opened them. "No. I wish I could say that. But I can't. The last thing I was thinking about before I went to sleep was...James Bond."

Logan's eyes narrowed. "I'm not James Bond."

"I know. It sounds crazy. But when I saw you in the elevator, you reminded me of him...."

Maybe it will make more sense if I go back to the beginning."

As Logan listened to Daisy's story, laced liberally with data about Merlin's magic and Catskill folklore, he couldn't help being fascinated by the way her mind worked. At the same time, her leaps of logic and flights of fancy had him feeling as if he'd suddenly been swept up into a whirlwind. A sensation not unlike the one he'd had when he'd made love to her.

A magic bed that promised true love? His gaze wandered past her to the object in question. For a second he thought he heard that strange music again. Ridiculous!

He didn't need magic or a centuries-old bed transported by some kind of Celtic mumbo jumbo. He had a much simpler explanation for what had happened in that bed last night. He shifted his gaze back to Daisy.

He'd wanted her almost from the first moment he'd seen her. He wanted her again right now. He wanted to unwrap her from that coverlet, carry her into the bedroom, lay her on that bed and make love to her until she never thought of Phillip again. Or of James Bond.

If she mentioned their names one more time... Logan's hands closed into fists where they rested on his thighs.

"You must think I'm crazy. And Phillip will never understand. I never even told him that the bed was magic or why I really wanted him to come up here with me."

Logan willed his body to relax. "All you have to do is tell him what you've told me. You wanted the whole enchilada—a socially advantageous marriage, one your aunt and uncle would approve of, and true love, to boot. Phillip should be able to get that much."

"What about the part where I tell him I made love with you instead? Oh my…" Daisy glanced over her shoulder at the bed, then back at Logan. "I just thought…we made love in that bed. What if we fall in love with each other?"

Logan looked her straight in the eye. "I don't believe in love." Then he rose and turned to add more wood to the fire.

"Somebody really hurt you," Daisy said softly.

"They did me a favor," Logan said. "Anyone who believes in love is a fool."

Daisy studied him as he fixed the fire. She could sense that he was angry. She'd seen it in his eyes just before he'd turned away. And for the first time, it occurred to her that she was alone in a cabin with a man she didn't know. She thought of her first impression of him in the elevator. *Dangerous.* Logan Campbell was a man capable of violence. She was sure of it, and yet she wasn't afraid of him.

She thought of his tenderness toward her during the night, his kindness even now. And she recalled the sense of connection she'd felt from that first moment.

Yet the man who turned to face her was a complete stranger. And she'd just spent the night making love with him.

Daisy rose from the couch. "Who are you, Logan Campbell, and why are you here?"

Logan pushed himself away from the mantel. "It's a long story. And I found that the refrigerator is well stocked. Why don't we have some breakfast first?"

"I don't cook," Daisy said.

"You can watch then," Logan said as he led the way to the kitchen.

And watch was exactly what Daisy did. Within minutes she had Logan Campbell pegged as a pro. The ease with which he gathered ingredients and utensils, the economy and grace of his movements as he sliced and diced, all testified to the fact that he was perfectly at home in a kitchen.

But then, Logan seemed to have an ability to fit into his surroundings wherever he went, Daisy decided. Yesterday, he'd looked as if he belonged on Wall Street. Today, she could have sworn he was a short-order cook. She was growing more curious by the moment. Who was he?

"You've worked as a chef, haven't you?"

Logan broke an egg into a bowl with one hand. "The actual job title was cook." Glancing up, he said, "You're very perceptive."

"I still haven't *perceived* why you followed me up here."

"Persistent, too." He focused his attention on whipping the eggs.

"But not patient," Daisy said. Logan didn't reply, but she saw the corners of his mouth twitch before he turned to the stove.

"After we eat," he said.

Maybe it was that hint of a smile, or perhaps it was the warmth of the sunlight splashing through the windows, but Daisy found herself relaxing.

It seemed the most natural thing in the world to be sitting at the counter watching a man in jeans and cowboy boots preparing an omelette. He had his sleeves rolled up, cracking eggs with one hand as if it was something he did every day.

She watched his fingers as they sprinkled herbs into the pan, then gripped a spoon and stirred. She could remember the way those lean, elegant hands had moved over her skin...the patterns they had traced, the response they had drawn. Something hot curled into a fist in her stomach. She could picture herself taking Logan by those hands and leading him back to the bed.

What would it be like to make love with him when they were both fully awake?

"Daisy?"

She blinked and raised her eyes to Logan's. He was studying her intently. "What?" she asked.

"Could you bring the plates and forks? The omelettes are ready."

He was a stranger, Daisy reminded herself as she gathered the required items and delivered them to the table. He had followed her to a secluded cabin, and he hadn't yet explained why. She had to get a grip.

But the thought slipped away the moment she took the first bite. That was when she realized she was starved. He'd put something in the omelettes to make them hot and spicy. Delicious.

"I'll bet you're from the Southwest," she said between bites.

"Years ago," he said.

"Delores, our cook, makes eggs like these. She was raised in Texas. Is that where you're from?"

Logan set his fork down. "Where I'm from is irrelevant."

Folding her hands, Daisy smiled at him. "Then why don't you tell me why you're here? As far as I'm concerned, that's relevant."

"I'm a private investigator, and I occasionally do work for Hanover Securities. Ten days ago, Phillip Baldwin asked me to find a missing person, an attorney named Eddie Maplethorpe. What do you know about him?"

"Maplethorpe? That was the name of the attorney who drew up Aunt Angela's last will."

"Didn't you think it was odd that your aunt would hire someone like him? Someone in a one-man office in Brooklyn? Wouldn't she have been more likely to use an attorney connected with Hanover Securities or at least with Wall Street?"

Daisy shook her head. "She went to a great deal of trouble to keep that will a secret. If Uncle Daniel had gotten wind of it, he would have tried to talk her out of it. When Mr. Maplethorpe first brought it to the house, Uncle Daniel threatened to contest it, but I managed to talk him out of that."

"Why?" Logan asked.

"Because it would have driven a wedge between him and his daughter. Stevie needs him right now."

"And if he contested the will, you stood to lose your two-million-dollar inheritance, didn't you?"

"I suppose. But that's not why... Oh." Tilting her head, Daisy studied him for a minute. "I can see it would appear that I might have had ulterior motives."

"Did you help your aunt find Mr. Maplethorpe?"

"No." Daisy frowned. "What exactly are you investigating me for, Mr. Campbell?"

"I want to know what your relationship was with Eddie Maplethorpe."

For a moment Daisy simply stared at Logan. "I'd never met the man before he came to the house to read the will."

"And you have no idea why your fiancé hired me to track him down?"

"No."

Logan studied her. If she was lying, she was very good at it. "Yesterday morning, Eddie Maplethorpe was killed by a hit-and-run driver. I don't believe it was an accident."

"Killed?" Daisy stared at him. "That's terrible. But I don't see..." Suddenly, she sprang from her chair. "You can't be serious. You think I had something to do with it? That I ran down Eddie Maplethorpe with my car? I don't know whether to laugh or to... C'mon."

Grabbing his hand, she pulled him with her, releasing him only to grasp the doorknob. "There's one sure way to find out. We can look at my car." Leading the way, she dragged him down the steps into the lean-to.

"Okay." She waved a hand as she circled to the front of the car. "You're the P.I. Go to it. Find something that proves I ran down…"

Daisy let the sentence trail off as she stared at the large dent in her grate. She couldn't for the life of her think of one thing to say as she watched Logan run his hand along it. It was two feet long and a foot wide.

"How did it happen?" Logan finally asked.

Daisy shivered. Though the wind from the night before had stilled, she felt as if it was cutting through her right to the bone. "I have no idea. I didn't even know the dent was there."

"You drove your car all the way into the city and then up here, and you never saw this dent?"

"I keep the car in the garage." She made herself walk to the rear, then back to the driver's door. "I can't see the front from here. And I didn't see it when I parked the car in Manhattan either."

"When was the last time you drove it?"

Daisy thought for a minute. "I'm not sure. I walk to the bookstore every day. It's only a mile and a half. I know how this must look, but I—"

"Anybody drive it besides you?"

"My cousin Stevie uses it. And Delores, our cook, uses it sometimes to get groceries. The spare keys are kept on a hook by the kitchen door. Maybe Delores or Stevie had an accident and was afraid to mention it."

Logan lowered himself to the ground, then began to wiggle backward under the front of the car.

Moving closer, Daisy leaned down. "What are you looking for?"

"Do you keep a flashlight in the car?"

"I'll get it." Daisy scrambled into the front seat, extracted it from the glove compartment, then placed it in his outstretched hand.

A few moments later, Logan inched his way out. He had a shred of cloth in his hand. A button dangled from it. The fragment looked as if it belonged to someone's suit jacket.

"You're some P.I.," Daisy said as her teeth began to chatter.

"Yeah, I'm the best. C'mon," Logan said as he took her arm and urged her back into the cabin. Seconds later, she was wrapped in the coverlet and sitting on the couch. Logan was adding more wood to the fire, and the shred of cloth was lying on the coffee table between them. Daisy couldn't take her eyes off it.

There was a definite downside to being a Bond girl. You ran the risk of becoming a murder suspect. In her mind, she pictured being handcuffed and shoved into a police car, then sitting in the witness stand, and finally rising to face a jury of her peers as they pronounced the verdict.

She heard something then. Not the music she'd heard earlier. This was louder, more like the muffled roar of an engine.

Did the electric chair make that much noise? she wondered.

Glancing up, she saw Logan grab a pair of binoculars off the mantel and head for the door. The noise was already growing fainter.

"A helicopter," he said as he returned and sat down on the coffee table to face her. "They're probably overseeing the crews working on the roads. It's a good sign. We may be able to get out of here soon."

Daisy drew in a deep breath. "I didn't run down Eddie Maplethorpe with my car."

"Did you ask Phillip to find him?"

"No. You must have misunderstood Phillip."

"And Phillip could have driven your car?"

"You can't suspect him." Daisy tried to get up, but Logan grabbed her arms and held her still.

"Stop trying to protect him. Eddie Maplethorpe was run down sometime between midnight and 3:00 a.m. Friday morning. Can you account for your whereabouts?"

Daisy stared at him. "I was in bed."

"Can anyone confirm that?"

"No, I don't suppose—"

"That's your car out there. If that piece of cloth can be connected to Eddie Maplethorpe, the police are going to list you as their prime suspect."

"Phillip wouldn't..."

Logan tightened his grip on her arms. "Does he mean that much to you? He didn't have any problem telling me that you were the one who wanted Maplethorpe found. What if he tells that to the police?"

Daisy opened her mouth, and then shut it. Finally, she said, "He's lying."

"I figured," Logan said.

"But he doesn't have any reason for wanting Maplethorpe dead."

"He has two million reasons, the same two million he had for marrying you."

Daisy met his eyes squarely. "You don't have a very high opinion of Phillip, but he didn't ask me to marry him for my money. We got engaged before Aunt Angela died, before I became an heiress."

"And then a will suddenly appeared to change all that," Logan said grimly.

"You think the will was a fake?" Daisy asked.

Logan sighed. "I'm thinking a lot of things. But I don't have any proof. Maybe your Uncle Daniel wanted Maplethorpe found, and Phillip was lying to protect him." He glanced down at the table. "Hell, I'm not even sure that this piece of cloth belongs to Maplethorpe. But I have a strong hunch that it does, and that your Phillip is involved up to his neck."

Daisy didn't say a thing, not even when Logan rose. All she could do was stare at the shred of cloth on the coffee table.

"Look," he said, "as far as I can tell, the road out there leads to this cabin and nowhere else. I don't imagine the plows will bother with it for some time. I'm going to chop more wood."

For some time after Logan left, Daisy sat staring into the fire. "At least he doesn't suspect *you* of murdering Eddie Maplethorpe," the little voice in her head said.

But if her car had been used to get rid of the attorney, then all the other people in her family who had access to it were suspects. And Logan was right, Phillip might have lied to protect Uncle Daniel.

Suddenly she stood up and threw off the coverlet. She was being ridiculous. Uncle Daniel couldn't have been involved in creating a fake will. He'd wanted to contest it. No one in her family could have had anything to do with Eddie Maplethorpe's murder. If it *was* murder. They didn't even know for sure yet if her car had done the deed. And everyone was innocent until proven guilty. With that thought uppermost in her mind, Daisy headed out to the kitchen.

While Logan was chopping wood, she would clean up. Her mind always seemed to work better when her hands were busy.

She was halfway through the dishes when she realized that she was spending more time watching Logan Campbell than she was cleaning up. First he'd shoveled a path out to the woodpile. Now he was chopping kindling. The hood of his jacket was down, and the front of it was open. He looked perfectly at home raising that ax, then swinging it down. Daniel Boone. It occurred to Daisy again that Logan Campbell looked very much at home doing anything.

It was then that she saw the bright flash of light from the woods beyond the woodpile. Narrowing her eyes, she looked for it again.

Several seconds passed. It was so quiet that she could hear Logan's ax each time it struck a piece of wood. Then she saw it again, light reflected off metal. Wiping her hands quickly, she raced to the fireplace, grabbed the binoculars, then ran back to the kitchen window.

It took her a few moments to focus, then she saw it. Someone was out there in the woods all right. He was carrying a rifle. She saw him slowly raise it—

With fear arrowing through her, Daisy raced to the kitchen door and dragged it open. "Logan, get down! Get down!"

Then she watched in horror as Logan bent low and began to run toward her. He was almost to the door when she felt the flash of heat near her cheek and heard the splinter of wood inches away. The sting in her arm came at the same moment Logan tackled her at the waist and fell with her to the kitchen floor.

4

LOGAN HEARD a third bullet hit wood with a dull *whack* just before he landed on top of Daisy on the floor.

"Are you all right?" he muttered as he shifted only enough to kick the kitchen door shut.

"Yes."

Her voice was breathless, barely a whisper. He kept her beneath him as he shrugged out of his jacket, then grabbed his gun from the back of his jeans. "We don't have much time. Tell me what you saw."

"A man...with...a rifle."

"Where?"

"In the...woods."

He cupped her chin with his free hand. Her eyes were open, fixed on his. He couldn't see a trace of fear in them. "Aren't you afraid?"

"Petrified. But I figure you must have a plan. James Bond always did."

"Yeah. Well, I'm not James Bond. Stay put." Rolling from her, he crawled to the door, then rose slowly, keeping out of sight as he scanned the yard. There was no sign of tracks in the snow. Not a flicker of movement in the woods beyond. "He can't come any closer without being seen," Logan said as his mind raced. "His best bet would be to circle to the other side of the cabin where the trees offer more cover. That should buy us a little time."

"Who...?" Daisy asked.

"Who knows you're up here?"

"Who knows *you're* up here? He was aiming his gun at you."

Logan turned to her. "You want to argue about which one of us he was trying to—" He froze, staring at her arm. "You're bleeding!"

Returning to her side, Logan swore as he stripped off his shirt and tore it into strips. Then he gently began to blot away the blood. It was only a scrape. The bullet hadn't entered her flesh, but already the skin was beginning to bruise. Fury moved through him, then twisted into a knot in his stomach.

"It doesn't hurt. Shouldn't it hurt?" Daisy asked.

The faintness of her voice had the anger surging up again. Ruthlessly, Logan pushed down the emotion. He gripped her chin, forcing it up. "Don't you dare faint on me."

Daisy closed her eyes, then opened them. She tried swallowing. "I never faint."

"Right. Try thinking about something else. A plan would be good since you seem to be big on them," Logan muttered as he began to turn the strips of his shirt into a pressure bandage. Antiseptic would have to wait until later.

He was tying it in place when she said, "If you climb out the bedroom window, you can waylay him in the woods, ambush him. What do you think?"

"What if he makes a surprise attack through one of the doors?"

"Good point," Daisy said. "What do we do then?"

Under other circumstances, he might have been flattered by the confidence he saw in her eyes. No one had ever looked at him in quite that way before. But under the present circumstances, he couldn't let her depend on him. "Your plan is a good one. It just needs some embellishing. I'll go out the window, and you'll hold down the fort."

Picking up his gun, he placed it in her hand, closing her fingers around it. "And you'll use this if you have to." For the first time, he saw a flicker of fear in her eyes. Satisfaction warred with guilt as he turned and made his way back to the kitchen door. Rising slowly and keeping out of sight, he scanned the yard. There was still no sign of the sniper. Locking it, he turned back to Daisy, who hadn't moved. She was staring at the gun.

"C'mon," he said as he moved past her into the living room. Working quickly, he threw the latch on the front door, then flipped over the couch. When he had it angled so that she could use it to shield herself against an attack from either door, he drew her down and settled her in front of him. Then he showed her how to hold the gun with both hands.

"This is the trigger." Leaning closer, he curled her finger around it. "All you have to do is squeeze. If you don't hit him the first time, squeeze again. At this distance, you'll have a good chance." Then he showed her how to use the back of the couch to steady her aim.

Until she turned to face him, he wasn't aware of how close she was, so close that all he could see was her eyes. And he was in them, in those sea-green depths. Whatever he was going to say slipped away. For a moment, all Logan could think about was Daisy. More than anything, he wanted to touch her. Really touch her while they were both wide-awake. He wanted to run his hands over every inch of her, to explore that soft, smooth skin until it grew warm and damp again. To feel that taut, agile body move beneath his. To sink into that heat.

Suddenly, it was imperative, essential, that he find out if his memories of last night were real. And this time, he wanted to see her eyes open and on his when he entered her. He wanted her to say his name.

Her eyes had darkened. Her breath was warm on his lips. All he had to do was draw her closer, just a matter of inches. He felt the pull. Not only from her. It was something inside of him... needing...yearning...

A log snapped and settled in the fireplace.

Daisy and Logan sprang apart.

"Think you can handle the gun?" Logan asked abruptly.

Daisy nodded. "I'm going to pray that I don't have to."

"Yeah. Well, just remember I'm not James Bond, and you may be on your own, kid. Squeeze that trigger if you have to." He was surprised at the effort it took to move away. He blocked her from his mind, blocked everything from his mind but what he had to do. Retrieving his jacket from the kitchen, he slipped into it, and pulled a knife from his boot. Crouching low, he made his way quickly into the bedroom.

Daisy held on to the gun for dear life as she heard the scrape of the window in the bedroom sliding up and then down.

He was gone. She was on her own. Her lungs were burning for air when she finally remembered to breathe.

How could she have forgotten something as simple, as basic, as that? she wondered as she drew in a second breath and released it.

Because of Logan Campbell. Just moments ago when he'd looked into her eyes, she'd forgotten everything but him. Suddenly, her entire universe had narrowed to one person. Oh, she'd read about it happening in books—the cliché about the earth stopping or tilting on its axis.

But what she'd experienced looking into Logan Campbell's eyes had been a first for her. For a moment, she could have sworn that time actually had stood still. The desire she'd seen in his eyes had been so intense. It was as if she were the only woman in the world he would ever want that much.

Was that what it would mean to be someone's soul mate? Was it possible that the bed had indeed cast its spell exactly as the Web site had promised?

No! Absolutely not! Daisy gulped in more air, praying that the oxygen would cool her blood and fuel her brain. There wasn't enough magic in the world to change Logan Campbell into her soul mate.

They were just too different. He was an adventurer, roaming the world, tracking down people. The only thing Daisy Hanover had ever roamed was the World Wide Web. Logan Campbell made gourmet omelettes; she had trouble boiling an egg. He went around armed to the teeth; the closest thing to a weapon she'd ever carried was a can of environmentally safe hair spray.

Until today. Daisy stared at the gun she held, ready to fire. There was no denying it. The evidence spoke for itself. Ever since she'd met Logan Campbell, she'd been changing slowly into a Bond girl.

A Bond girl whose trigger finger was falling asleep! Slowly, she relaxed her death grip on the handle of the revolver and began to shake the needles out of her right hand. She could worry about Logan and magic later. Right now, she'd better concentrate on a sniper who might come barreling through the door at any moment. After flexing her hand a few more times, Daisy gripped the gun again and listened.

She couldn't hear a thing. The wind from the night before had stilled. Even the fire was dying out.

Quiet was good, she reminded herself. Unless the sniper was using a silencer.

Her hands started to shake. Quickly, she rested them on the couch. And then the thought struck her. Logan had left the gun with her. He was unarmed. Fear bubbled up until it lodged like a hard fist in her throat. It was then that she heard it—the crunch of snow under someone's foot.

Shoving the terror aside, Daisy crouched lower, bringing her head down just the way Logan had showed her. Then she counted the seconds. One...two...

She was at five when she heard a board creak on the front porch. She had to bite down hard on her lip to keep from screaming.

It wasn't Logan. It couldn't be him. Surely he would have shouted a warning. Something. Her arms felt frozen. Taking a deep breath, she gripped the gun tighter. Closing one eye, she concentrated on lining up her shot, the way they did on TV cop shows.

Another board creaked. Daisy squeezed her finger on the trigger.

The blast roared through the cabin, the glass in the window shattered.

"Damn it! Hold your fire and open this door. It's me," Logan shouted.

Scrambling to her feet, Daisy raced to the door and made quick work of the latch. The moment it swung open, she launched herself at Logan. "Are you all right?"

"I'm fine," Logan assured her, holding her tight. It was only then that Daisy began to tremble. For a second, the fear that she'd held in check threatened to explode within her. Tightening her grip on him, she said, "Did you...is he...?"

"He got away. I tracked him partway to the highway, but he was wearing snowshoes. I

couldn't keep up." As he spoke, Logan drew her
with him into the cabin and shut the door. "I
don't think he'll be back, but we have to get out
of here. C'mon, I want to fix that arm first." He
led her to the bedroom.

"My arm's fine," Daisy said as he boosted her
onto the bed and disappeared into the bathroom.

"I'm going to make sure of that."

Daisy glanced at the first-aid kit in Logan's
hand when he came back into the room, then
wiggled back farther on the bed. "It could start
bleeding all over again if you remove the bandage."

"That's all right. I don't faint at the sight of
blood." He sat down beside her.

"Maybe I do."

Raising one eyebrow, Logan said, "Funny,
but when you were holding that gun, you didn't
look like a coward."

"I'm not." Her eyes suddenly narrowed.
"Don't you dare laugh at me."

"I'm not," Logan said, taking her arm and un-
fastening the knot he'd tied earlier.

"I saw your lips twitch." Daisy said, then
winced as he applied a liberal amount of something that burned so much it brought tears to her
eyes. "Ouch!"

"And you claim you aren't a coward," Logan
said as he applied fresh gauze and secured it
with tape.

"You're lucky I don't still have that gun,"
Daisy muttered.

This time when his lips twitched, the smile lit

his eyes too. And Daisy found herself staring. For a second, she could have sworn that the whole room brightened. Maybe it had, or maybe she just hadn't noticed before that the sun was splashing through the windows, gleaming off the dark wood of the bed.

Quite suddenly, she was aware of everything. The way his fingers tightened, one by one on the sensitive underside of her arm. The way his eyes were darkening now, as swiftly as the summer sky faded to black before a storm.

Only the storm wasn't only in his eyes. She could feel it building in her too. Something wild and fierce ached to break free. And she simply didn't care. All she had to do was move forward, press her mouth to his and she could know once and for all if what she remembered of the night they'd spent together had been real, or if she'd only imagined it. And she had to know. She simply couldn't go on without knowing.

Slowly, inexorably, they moved toward each other until their mouths were touching.

It hadn't been a dream. It was the one solid thought he could grasp in the flood of emotions moving through him. Logan couldn't identify them all. There were too many, and the analytical part of his mind was already shutting down. Her skin, impossibly smooth beneath his fingers, was already heating, and her lips were so soft they were melting beneath his.

He had to taste her. Just once, he promised himself. Just to make sure that he hadn't imagined that either. But as he began to explore her mouth and the sinfully sweet flavor poured through him, he knew he'd lied. This was something he'd longed for, something he would always crave. One taste would never be enough. His hand was already moving to the back of her head to urge her closer. Even as he changed the angle of the kiss to take it deeper, he knew that she was pulling something from him. He didn't seem to have any defense against it. He could hear the faint sound of music, not a melody so much as a beat that seemed to match the pulsing of his own blood. Or hers. And with it came needs. He wanted to touch her. He had to. Just once. He brought his hand up in one smooth stroke along her thigh, over her hip to settle over her breast.

Greed came so swiftly. Daisy felt utterly helpless as it took command. No man had ever touched her this way. No one had ever made her feel this desperate. She knew with deep certainty that no one ever would.

Suddenly she wanted more than his kiss, more than his hard hand pressed against her, and much more than his dark unsettling flavor filling her. Moving her hands to his shoulders, she grabbed fistfuls of his jacket and dragged it down his arms. His T-shirt came next as she curled her fingers into it and ripped. She didn't want any barriers between them. She craved that flood of feelings that he'd brought her during the night. She wanted him. Only him.

Logan was struggling for breath when he drew back. Her lips were parted, still damp from his kiss. Her eyes were the dark-green color of a storm-tossed sea. His jacket was off, his chest naked. She'd torn his T-shirt just as she'd ripped something out of him. In another moment he feared she might have everything.

It was that thought only that kept Logan from finishing what they'd started. Still neither of them spoke. Finally, Logan broke the silence. "This is…I've never…I…" No woman had ever made him stutter.

Daisy drew in a deep breath. "Me, too. It's got to be the bed. I think it really has cast some kind of spell on us."

Logan frowned. "I told you before. I don't believe in love. And magic only exists in books, or in very fertile imaginations."

"I'm not making it up," Daisy said. "According to the Web site, this bed can trace its powers back to Merlin."

"Merlin derives his very existence from a book. He's a story somebody made up in his head. Case closed."

Daisy poked a finger into his chest. "Well, just now when you kissed me, I call that magic. I mean, you were…no one has ever made me feel that way. I wanted, well, you had to know what I wanted. And you wanted it too. Just try to tell me that you didn't." Pausing, she studied him for a moment. "Or maybe it wasn't the same for you."

Logan stared at her. He'd never known another woman who said everything that was on her mind. She couldn't possibly be that naive, or that honest, could she? He wanted her now even more than he had a few moments ago. All he was certain of was that if he touched her...

"I can see that it wasn't." Blushing furiously, Daisy edged to the side of the bed.

Logan grabbed her good arm and held her still. He should let her go on thinking what she was thinking. Maybe then he'd be able to keep his hands off her. If she hated him, maybe, just maybe, he could think of something besides making love to her again on the damn bed. "What you said. I'll go along with it."

"Oh," Daisy said and blinked.

"But that doesn't mean we're under some kind of magical spell. There's another explanation for what we're feeling. Lust. Pure and simple."

Daisy sighed. In relief, she was sure of it. "Right. Lust. Pure and simple. Of course. I was worried there for a minute. But we couldn't fall in love. Think of it. You and me, soul mates? The whole idea is impossible."

"Impossible," Logan said. But it wasn't relief he was feeling. It was annoyance. And for a moment, he had an overwhelming urge to push her down on the bed and kiss her again until she couldn't think of anything or anyone but him. But it would be a mistake. He glanced at the headboard, at the supposedly Celtic inscription she'd pointed out to him earlier. No, the whole damn thing was impossible.

When he glanced back at Daisy, she was beaming a smile at him. "I was really worried. But I think I've got it figured out now. I did some reading about magic. It's very dependent on the power of suggestion. That must be what's going on here. I was actually starting to think…" Pausing, she leaned a little closer to him. "Last night, I even imagined that I heard music. I thought it must be magic because I couldn't identify the tune or the instrument. Did you hear it?"

"No," Logan said with a quick shake of his head. "I didn't hear anything."

"There, you see? It must have been some kind of self-hypnosis. I was sure I heard music. I was even going to check around for the wires." She glanced around the room.

"There aren't any," Logan said.

Daisy's eyes narrowed as they met his. "I thought you said you didn't hear music."

"Checking for wires is something a P.I. does automatically. It's instinctive," Logan lied glibly as he reached for his jacket and pulled it on.

"Speaking of P.I.s, that reminds me. I figured out a plan while you were chopping the wood. It will solve both our problems. I want to hire you."

Logan stared at her. Was he ever going to get used to the way her mind worked? "You want to hire me? For what?"

Daisy smiled. "To track down Eddie Maplethorpe's killer—if he *was* killed. What do you charge?"

"I'm already tracking down Maplethorpe's killer. And I'm looking at the prime suspect right now."

"That's the beauty of my plan," Daisy explained. "As the only suspect so far, I want

Eddie's killer found as much as you do. I know I didn't run him down. But if you turn over what you know to the police, I'm not going to be able to explain that dent in my car or that piece of cloth you found. I figure if I hire you, all that becomes confidential information."

"Forget it. I don't take bribes, and there is no P.I.-client privilege."

"The P.I.s in books are always loyal to their clients," Daisy argued.

"That's fiction. This is real life."

Daisy's chin lifted. "All right, forget loyalty and privilege. We still have a common goal. We both want to find out who killed Eddie Maplethorpe. It'll save time if we work together. I could even help you investigate the case. I used to be a research librarian before I opened my bookstore. I bet I could make a pretty good P.I. And I think we should postpone turning over my car to the police until we've had a chance to examine all the evidence."

Logan studied her for a moment. "You can save yourself some time and money. I'm already pretty sure you didn't do it. I have a hunch who did."

Daisy grabbed his arm as he slid off the bed. "I still want to hire you. Name your fee."

Until that moment, Logan didn't know that jealousy could cut like a knife. "Your fiancé means that much to you?"

"Phillip is family. He's been so good for Uncle Daniel—and for my cousin. If it hadn't been for him, I'm not sure any of us could have gotten through my aunt's death. I know that he couldn't have killed Mr. Maplethorpe."

Even as the knife twisted in his gut, Logan said, "He had access to your car."

"Anyone in my family could have used it. But they didn't. Not to run down Eddie Maplethorpe. You've got to help me prove that."

Logan could see everything in her eyes. The love, the loyalty—and shining through them was something else. Joan of Arc might have looked that way as she led her French troops into battle. Once again, he tried to identify the feelings that moved through him. Envy. Longing. Pity. "Be very careful. Your family can betray you, as easily as a stranger can."

"I can't believe that," Daisy said.

Without thinking, Logan reached out to tuck a strand of hair behind her ear. The words were out before he could stop them. "This isn't a story. I can't promise you a happy ending. And you can't buy my silence. If one of them turns out to be the killer, we hand them over to the police."

Daisy drew in a deep breath and let it out. "Agreed. You're going to take my offer, aren't you?"

He nodded slowly. "One more thing. I'm the boss."

He made it to the fireplace before she stopped him, grabbing his arm and pulling him around. "How do you figure that? I'm writing the check."

Logan's lips twitched. "The check only buys

you the privilege of following orders. Take it or leave it."

Daisy reluctantly shook his outstretched hand. "What's your plan?"

Logan took his cell phone out of his pocket. "I'm going to make a quick call to my office to get things started, and then we're going to hike up to the main road and head back to the city."

5

IT DIDN'T LOOK like the office of a successful private investigator.

That was Daisy's first assessment when Logan ushered her into the small two-room suite on Manhattan's Upper West Side. The furnishings could only be described as early Sam Spade. A six-foot slab of wood atop two file cabinets served as a desk, and the mismatched chairs looked as if they'd been discarded by earlier tenants. The place could have been a movie set for a forties detective film except for the state-of-the-art computer and the ponytailed young man seated in front of it. He was definitely out of place. He should have been a frizzy-haired blond woman wearing a suit that fit like a second skin.

Logan Campbell didn't seem to belong in the room either. He was too…competent-looking.

Daisy let her gaze sweep the room a second time. A Bond girl wouldn't be caught dead here.

"Daisy Hanover, this is Ray Juarez, my assistant," Logan said as the man with the ponytail rose.

"Miss Hanover."

"Daisy, please." She found her hand grasped firmly by Ray, whose worn jeans contrasted with his button-down shirt and tie. He was in his mid-to late twenties, she guessed. In addition to the ponytail, he wore a gold earring and sported a tattoo on his left forearm.

"Daisy's got a stake in the Maplethorpe case. She needs to sign a contract and write us a check," Logan said.

Seconds later, Daisy found herself seated at the far end of the desk skimming through two single-spaced pages of legal mumbo jumbo. Out of the corner of her eye, she saw that Logan had settled one hip on the slab of wood to listen to Ray's report. As she eavesdropped on their conversation, she realized three things. First, Eddie Maplethorpe's death was only one of the cases Campbell Investigations was handling. Second, Logan valued his assistant's input. And third, she'd been wrong in her first impression that Logan seemed out of place in this office. Leaning back against the wall, swinging one booted foot as Ray handed him something to sign, Logan had begun to look very much at home. In a wrinkled trench coat and hat, he could have passed for Sam Spade.

It occurred to her yet again that Logan Campbell had an amazing ability to adapt to his surroundings. As she reached for a pen and signed the contract and then a check, a series of images flashed through her mind. Logan looking like James Bond in the elevator. Logan making omelettes in the kitchen and chopping wood as if those were chores he performed every day.

And last night in that bed? Well, he'd slipped perfectly into that role too. The lover of her dreams. Placing her pen carefully on the desk, Daisy turned to stare at him.

Who was Logan Campbell? Then suddenly she was distracted by the names Logan and Ray were talking about, and she shot out of the chair. Logan Campbell, whoever he was, had operatives assigned to everyone in her family.

Walking up to him, she pinned him with a look. "Why are you following my niece and uncle?"

"Either one of them could have borrowed your car that night."

"But they would never have used it to run down Eddie Maplethorpe," Daisy said.

"Maybe not. But there's a sniper on the loose. Until we find him, I'm going to keep everyone under surveillance."

"Do you think they're in danger?"

"I'm just doing my job. When you signed that contract, you gave me free rein to run this investigation any way I see fit." Logan turned back to Ray. "What about Baldwin?"

"We haven't been able to locate him," Ray said. "The operative waited for him to come out of the Hanover Building until almost eight o'clock last night. The night guard at the desk thought he was working late, but he wasn't in his office when they checked. He hasn't been seen entering or leaving his apartment, and so far, no one has spotted him at the Hanover estate."

"Phillip's missing?" Daisy asked.

"Unless he's holed up in his apartment and not answering the phone," Ray said.

Daisy turned to Logan. "I want to hire you to find him. Should I write another check?"

"You've already written me a check to find him," Logan said.

Daisy fisted her hands on her hips. "You can't still think he's the one who ran down Maplethorpe and then hired a gunman to shoot at you this morning. He's missing! Something might have happened to him."

Logan grabbed Daisy's shoulders. "Maybe he realized after our little discussion yesterday afternoon that the jig was up. Maybe he's decided to cut his losses and run."

"Why are you so determined to make Phillip the villain in all this?"

Logan's eyes narrowed. "He hired me to find Eddie Maplethorpe, then he lied to me and told me that you were the one who wanted Maplethorpe found, and now he's disappeared."

Daisy lifted her chin. "What if that sniper was expecting to find Phillip and me at the cabin? It wasn't a secret that we were going there. What if Phillip was the sniper's target all along? He could be in real danger!"

It was only when Ray cleared his throat that Logan realized he and Daisy were standing toe to toe. He felt how his hands were gripping her shoulders hard and knew it was because he was itching to fasten them around her neck. Jealousy. There was no other label for the emotion knifing through him. And there was nothing plain or simple about it. Just as there wasn't anything plain or simple about what he was feeling for Daisy. It was…complicated.

Ray cleared his throat again. "I have to leave now if I'm going to be in time for my class at Columbia."

Logan dropped his hands to his sides. "Go ahead. I'll look into Baldwin's whereabouts myself."

"There's coffee. I just brewed a fresh pot," Ray said as he slipped into a jacket and then an overcoat.

Daisy didn't speak until Ray closed the door behind him. "Thank you."

The knife Logan felt lodged inside of him twisted. "Don't thank me yet. You may not like what I find." Turning, he walked abruptly into the adjoining room. "I'm going to take a shower and change. Help yourself to coffee. Ray usually leaves sandwich stuff in the refrigerator."

She belongs to someone else. Logan repeated the words to himself over and over as he let the shower pound him. She'd slept with him because she'd been expecting her fiancé to show up. So it was Phillip she'd been thinking of. Or her fantasy lover, James Bond. Maybe she *had* to fantasize with Phillip Baldwin. The thought gave him a momentary feeling of comfort, but it faded the second he recalled the look in Daisy's eyes when she'd pleaded with him to find Phillip. She had feelings for him.

Stepping out of the small shower stall, Logan rubbed himself dry, then fastened the towel around his waist. She belonged to someone who at the very least might be marrying her for her money, and at the worst, might be setting her up to take the fall for a murder. But she was loyal.

And he was being stupid. Logan repeated the words in his mind as he turned to face himself in the small mirror over the sink. He was beginning to care for someone who cared for someone else. He'd made that mistake before. The only difference between Daisy Hanover and Lucy Farnsworth was that Daisy was being honest with him. She wasn't trying to disguise her feelings for Phillip Baldwin.

So he'd better do what he was good at. Finding people. The sooner he found Phillip Baldwin and answered the questions he had about Eddie Maplethorpe's death, the sooner he could distance himself from Daisy Hanover. Then his problem would be solved.

Logan held on to that belief for the entire time it took him to step out of the bathroom and into the room. Daisy was standing in the open door of his closet, examining his clothes.

As he watched, she lifted her hand, running it along the shoulder of one of his jackets, then down the sleeve. The gesture was so simple, so natural, and she looked so right doing it. For a moment, it was almost as if she belonged there, standing in his closet, picking out his clothes.

He never brought clients to his office. He'd never brought a woman to the place he lived in.

It had been a mistake to bring Daisy here.

It had been a mistake to turn around. Daisy realized it the moment she did it. His skin was damp, still gleaming with drops of water. And beneath was all lean muscle, pulled taut over long bones. He was beautiful. She felt the punch of desire hit her hard in her stomach, then again in her heart. Absolutely stunned, she felt numb and, at the same time, incredibly aware of everything about him, all at the same time.

A billow of steam had followed him into the room. She wasn't even aware that she'd moved closer, only that she could smell his shower, the soap he'd used on his skin. She could smell him. His hair was slicked back from his face, making his cheekbones more prominent and giving him the look of a warrior. She could picture him in a kilt, with a sword in his hand, the Highland mists surrounding him as he led his clan in a charge.

Daisy watched a drop of water fall from his hair, then slowly roll along a path from his shoulder down his chest to his... As it disappeared into the towel he'd hitched at his waist, she became paralyzed. Try as she might, she couldn't take her gaze away from that towel, couldn't even draw in a breath. And she definitely couldn't move her arms.

If she could, she would reach for the towel and rip it off. The image was so clear in her mind, just as clear as the wish in her heart. *Lust!* That's what Logan had called it. Lust, pure and simple.

She'd become its slave.

She stared, still not able to move or speak, as Logan's hands moved slowly to the towel. The breath she'd been holding whooshed out and she dragged in another as she wrenched her gaze from his hands to his face. It didn't help one bit! She recognized immediately what she saw in his eyes. Desire as dark, as desperate, as

her own. He was going to reach out to her and
touch her. She could already imagine his hands
on her. Then he would make love to her right
here on the floor, just as he had last night in that
bed. She could picture it so clearly....

And then as suddenly as if he'd switched off a
light, Logan's eyes became shuttered, his expression unreadable. Daisy knew without looking that he'd secured the towel at his waist. The
breath she'd been holding slipped out in a sigh.
Of relief, she told herself.

But she lied.

"What are you doing?" Logan asked.

Lusting. Daisy could only pray she hadn't said
the word aloud. What *had* she been doing just
before...? Ruthlessly, Daisy dragged her gaze
away from Logan and turned back to the closet.
"Research," she said. "I'm trying to figure out
who you are."

"By snooping through my clothes?"

Daisy felt the heat flood her cheeks, but she
didn't glance back. She wasn't going to risk
looking at him again until her pulse had steadied. "I was desperate. You're a man I've made
love with, a man I've hired to keep my family
and me from being arrested, and—"

"You've hired me to investigate Eddie Maplethorpe's death, with no strings attached."

"Whatever." Daisy waved a hand. "The point
is, I know very little about you. So I decided to
do a little research. But you don't keep anything
personal in your office, no books, no photos on
the desk."

"It's Ray's desk."

"Exactly. You don't even seem to have one. But *these* are your clothes." She pointed to a jacket. "You were wearing this on the elevator yesterday afternoon. And your closet door *was* open." Just a crack. She'd widened it considerably, and what she'd found had confirmed what she'd already suspected. Once again she glanced at the shelf with its neat array of hats, wigs and glasses, then at the clothes, carefully clustered into outfits. Costumes.

"What did you learn by snooping through my closet?" Logan asked.

"I prefer to call it research," Daisy said. "And I learned that you're not always James Bond."

"I'm *never* James Bond," Logan said.

Daisy lifted a hanger holding a tuxedo and turned to face him. "I'll bet you look just like him in this. I'll bet you even order your martinis shaken, not stirred, when you wear it. I fell in love with Sean Connery the first time I heard him say that."

Logan took the tuxedo from her and rehung it. "I drink beer." Then he selected black slacks and a matching turtleneck sweater.

Daisy nodded. "That's probably what all cat burglars drink."

Logan stared at her for a minute, and then his lips suddenly twitched. "You've researched the drinking habits of cat burglars?"

"I could. I was only guessing. But that's a cat burglar's costume you've picked, isn't it?" she said, looking at what he was holding. "Is that what we're going to do next? Break and enter Phillip's apartment?"

"*We're* not going to do anything. You're going to stay here while I do a little *research* in Phillip Baldwin's apartment." Turning, he started back to the bathroom.

"Now wait just a—" The rest of her thought flew right out of her mind when she saw the scars crisscrossing his back. The angry-looking marks were puckered, faded. But the pain slicing through her was fresh. She could almost see the whip lashing out, ripping through his flesh. In three quick strides she grabbed his arm and stopped him. "Your back...how? Who beat you?"

Logan studied her for a minute. What had happened that night years ago was something he never talked about. Not to anyone. "It was a long time ago."

"I can see that. I want to know who did it."

When he still said nothing, she gave his arm a hard shake. "Who?"

"The father of a woman who claimed I raped her."

He watched her eyes widen in shock, felt her hand go limp for just a second before she tightened her grip on his arm again. "She lied."

It wasn't a question. It was a simple statement of faith. A gift. He could see it in her eyes, feel it in the way her hands moved to grasp his. In the endless days he'd spent in jail, no one in his family had believed in him. No one had visited him.

"Why did she tell a lie like that?" Daisy asked.

"It's a long story," he said. "The woman was engaged to my brother. I didn't rape her, but I did sleep with her. You could argue that her father was justified in beating me, in sending me to jail. My parents felt he was."

"Your parents didn't stand up for you? They believed you were capable of rape? That's... that's terrible."

His hands gripped hers tightly. He couldn't have said what her words meant to him. But something inside of him, part of a wall he'd built within himself, shifted. And what moved through him then was fear. "No, that's life. Even your family can betray you." Disengaging her hands, he turned and walked into the bathroom.

For a moment, as Daisy stared at the door he closed behind him, thoughts and feeling swirled through her.

Who in the world was he? Whatever she'd guessed, whatever she'd discovered in his closet, it wasn't the whole picture. It was only a facade. The young man sitting in a jail cell, accused of a rape he hadn't committed, was a place to start. But Logan didn't want to talk about that.

Turning, she began to pace back and forth in the small room that adjoined Logan's office. The furniture—a couch, a table with a hot plate and a small refrigerator—lined one wall. A wall that cried out for a paint job. There was nothing else in the room, not a bookshelf or even a painting that offered a clue about Logan Campbell.

He was as much a missing person as the people he tracked down. Daisy stopped pacing. Of course, that was it. If she wanted to find the real Logan Campbell, she had the perfect opportunity to learn how to do it from a pro.

She glanced back at the bathroom door. A pro who had no intention of sharing his secrets or of taking her along on his cat-burgling caper. She'd just have to change his mind. As if he'd read hers, Logan stepped into the room.

Cat burglar didn't do him justice. The black turtleneck and slacks fit him like a second skin. He looked more like a member of a Ninja death squad.

When he tried to walk past her, Daisy stepped into his path. "I want to go with you."

"No." Logan moved around her into the next room.

She started after him. "But I can—" She stopped short to prevent a collision when he whirled suddenly to face her. "I can help," she told him. "Being a research librarian isn't a lot different from being a private eye. We're both trying to track something down."

Logan took her by the shoulders and gave her a little shake. "What a librarian tracks down doesn't shoot bullets at her. You saw that sniper this morning. That should be reason enough for you to stay here where you'll be safe. The next time, he might not miss."

Dropping his hands, Logan turned to the desk and opened a file drawer. Daisy hurried to the office door and put her back against it. She had a moment to brace herself as he slipped a leather pouch into his jacket. It wasn't long enough to prepare her for the quick flash of anger she saw when he looked up and his eyes met hers. Then her throat dried up and her stomach muscles quivered.

She'd sensed the temper that he buried beneath that steely control. But she'd never seen it this clearly before, savage, fierce, ready to leap out and devour her.

"We have an agreement, Daisy."

"I'm willing to abide by it." The words tumbled out, and if the door hadn't been at her back, she was almost sure she would have turned and run. "But we'll find Phillip faster if you take me with you."

"You'll only slow me down," Logan said, advancing on her.

"No. Think about it. I've known Phillip for almost a year. I've been to his apartment. I can tell you things, like if any clothes are missing from his closet. And…other things."

Logan stopped a foot away from her. Desperate, she played her trump card. "And you won't have to waste time picking the lock with whatever it is you've got in that pouch. I have a key."

"Hand it over," Logan said.

"It won't do you any good because Henry, the doorman, doesn't know you."

Logan studied her for a minute. Finally, he said, "There's a very good reason why I prefer to work alone. I don't have to argue with anyone."

Daisy raised two hands in a gesture of surrender. "I'll stop. If you take me with you, I won't say another word."

"And you'll follow orders," Logan warned as he took her arm and drew her away from the door.

"I swear," Daisy said, matching two steps to one of his as they hurried down the hall.

WITH ITS CABLES protesting every foot of the distance, the elevator groaned its way to the seventh floor. Logan stood close to Daisy, within reach of her. But he was very careful not to touch her. And he wasn't speaking either. Instead, he was counting silently to ten. It was something he'd learned to do as a child to hold his temper in check.

He couldn't recall the last time he'd had to resort to the tactic. Control over his emotions was something he'd achieved long ago. Because feelings interfered. They clouded your ability to see straight. To think straight. And in his business, they led to mistakes, sometimes fatal ones.

Daisy Hanover had been stirring up his feelings and dragging them out of him since they'd met.

When Logan got to ten, the elevator doors slid open, and he was still angry. At Daisy and at himself. He never should have brought her with him. As they stepped together into the narrow hall, he took Daisy's arm and turned her to face him. "There was no doorman. You lied."

"I was desperate. But you'll see. You won't be sorry that you brought me."

He tightened his grip on her arm, but he managed to keep his voice low. "You're going to be sorry if you lie to me again."

"Okay," she said. "Understood. What do we do next?"

"Which door?" Logan asked.

Daisy led the way down the hall. When they got to the door, Logan knocked and then waited. Finally, he turned to Daisy and said, "The key.

Or was that something else you made up because you were desperate?"

She dug it out of her pocket.

"When I tell you, unlock the door, then step to the side and wait." At her nod, he put his ear to the door and listened. But there was nothing. He couldn't even make out the murmur of a TV. Slipping his gun out, he signaled her to open the door. The moment she did, he took out his flashlight and, crouching low, swung it in an arc. There was no sign of movement.

"Wait here," he said as he stepped into the small foyer. The place had been ransacked. Furniture was overturned, books and papers littered the floor. Making his way through the rubble, he pointed his gun and the beam of his light through the bedroom door, then checked the adjoining bathroom. Nothing. The kitchen was galley-size, and it, too, was empty except for the debris strewn across the floor. It was then that he heard the sound and turned. Daisy was standing stock-still in the living room staring at the destruction.

"I told you to wait," Logan said, pocketing his flashlight and flipping the light switch.

"I…" Daisy took a deep breath and tried again. "What were they looking for?"

"Probably the same thing we are," Logan said as he moved quickly to close the apartment door and lock it. "Some hint about where Baldwin might be."

"Maybe he was here and whoever did this snatched him. Or…oh my God, is he…?"

She shot past him before he could stop her,

jumped over books, an overturned table. She had the light on in the bedroom when he caught up.

"He's not here," Logan said.

"The kitchen—"

Logan grabbed her this time and held her still. "He's not in the kitchen or the bathroom. I checked. Do you think I would have let you—"

"They could have killed him here and moved the body, right?"

Twin desires warred within him. Part of him wanted to wipe the look of fear from her eyes. Part of him wanted to shake her. Cursing Phillip Baldwin, Logan gathered her close as a tight fist of envy curled in his gut. Quickly, he scanned the room again. "There's no blood," he said.

"Blood?" Daisy pulled back so she could meet his eyes.

"If he was here and put up a fight, there might be blood."

Daisy shut her eyes, took a deep breath and opened them again. "We have to find him before they hurt him."

As she struggled to pull away, Logan went with his second impulse and gave her a shake. "Why are you so concerned about this guy? Doesn't it occur to you that if someone's after him, that means he's got to be involved in whatever is going on? Are you so much in love with him that you can't see straight?"

"No. I'm not in love with him at all." Placing her palms flat on his chest, she gave him a good shove. "But I agreed to marry him. You were absolutely right about me. I was greedy. I wanted the whole enchilada. That's why I wanted to take him up to that cabin and get him into that bed. It was supposed to fix everything. Instead, a sniper tried to shoot you because he probably thought you were Phillip, and now someone's trying to find Phillip so he can finish the job, and it's all my fault!"

Logan studied her for a minute. Trying to follow the way her mind worked was easier than trying to identify the emotions running through him. But it was still a challenge.

Finally, he said, "Get a grip. You can't blame yourself for this. There's no law against marrying a man you don't love. Women do that every day. And if someone *is* trying to kill Phillip, it's not because you tried to lure him into a magic bed. There's more going on here than that. And I'm betting that your Phillip is up to his ears in it."

Daisy frowned at him. "You don't even know him, and yet you're determined to think the worst of him. Why?"

"Because I know people. And I know what greed can do to them. The four million dollars that your aunt left to you and your cousin could make a saint greedy."

"I told you. Phillip proposed to me before my aunt died. Before he or I or anyone knew that I was an heiress."

"But Eddie Maplethorpe would have known," Logan said.

Daisy frowned. "I suppose."

"And your aunt would have known. She could have told someone."

"Yes, but—"

"What did you do with your money?" Logan asked.

"I left it invested at Hanover Securities. That's who was managing the money for my aunt, so I just signed some papers."

It was Logan's turn to frown. "What kind of papers?"

"Something that would allow Phillip to service my new account, instead of Uncle Daniel."

"So Phillip gets the commission for handling your money, and he gets to marry the heiress, to boot. Lucky for him that Eddie Maplethorpe showed up with that new will, isn't it?" Logan raised a hand to stop Daisy from interrupting. "Your problem is that you *do* know him, and you're determined to think the best of him. What would happen if you let that kind of bias color your research? The number-one rule of a good P.I. is to be objective."

Daisy stared at him for a minute. "Okay, you've got a point." For the first time since she entered the apartment, she summoned up a smile. "And I promised you wouldn't be sorry you brought me along." Drawing in a deep breath, she turned and let her gaze sweep the room. "Where do you want me to start?"

Logan studied her for a minute. If she was willing to concede her bias, perhaps it was time he admitted his. "Why don't we start in the kitchen. Maybe if we work together, we can cancel out each other's prejudices."

"Together?" Daisy beamed another smile at him as she extended her hand. "Like partners?

Did you ever notice how all the great fictional detectives have a partner, like Sherlock Holmes and Watson, Nero Wolfe and Archie, and all those inspectors from Scotland Yard have their police sidekicks."

He ignored her hand and started toward the bedroom. "Let's not get carried away. I just think we can be more objective if we search the place together. I never work with a partner."

"Yeah, I know," Daisy dropped her hand and began to pick her way through the rubble. "You're a loner like James Bond."

Logan clenched his teeth. "I'm not James Bond."

"If you say so," Daisy agreed amiably as she let her gaze sweep the narrow kitchen. "What do I look for?"

"Something that's out of place. Something that catches your eye. Anything that will tell us where Phillip might have gone."

"Everything's out of— Look!" Hurrying to the window, she pointed to a pane. "The sniper!"

Whirling, she launched herself at Logan, and fell with him to the floor.

6

THE MOMENT HE HIT the floor, Logan rolled, taking Daisy with him until they were clear of the doorway. Keeping her trapped beneath him, he waited for the sound of a shot.

When it didn't come, he risked a quick glance over his shoulder. The window was dark. No sign of movement. "What did you see?"

"The pane of glass...shattered."

In his mind, Logan played back his earlier, brief search of the kitchen. He'd been looking for a body. But that hadn't been why he'd missed the broken pane in the window. He hadn't seen it because Daisy had distracted him. Just as she was distracting him now. His entire body had hardened the instant she'd fallen on top of him. Now with every soft curve of her pressed beneath him in a perfect fit, he grew harder still. He knew the instant the tremor moved through her. He felt the echo of it right to his very core. No one, nothing had ever made him want this way.

With an oath, he rolled off her and drew in a deep breath. What the hell was the matter with him? If he believed in magic spells...

But he didn't. Gripping her chin, he turned her face to his. "You see anything else?"

"No."

"Then why the flying tackle?"

"You were standing right there in the doorway! A perfect target. I thought—"

"Stay here," he ordered. Keeping low, he crept along the wall until he reached the kitchen doorway. It was anger simmering in his blood now. Anger at himself. Because Daisy was right. They'd both have made perfect targets if someone was out there watching the apartment. Shoving his emotions down, he drew his gun and turned into the room, edging along the wall until he realized he was aiming his weapon at a brick wall. Then he spotted the fire escape. Opening the window slowly, he checked it. It was empty except for a cat, scratching at the window on the level above. Pulling himself back in, he closed the window, then tucked his gun back into his waistband. "All clear."

"How can you be sure there's not a sniper out there in a darkened room, lining up his shot?" Daisy asked.

"This window looks out on a brick wall. And snipers don't normally hang out on fire escapes. They keep their distance and use a telescopic lens." He ran his fingers along the wood that had framed the missing glass. "It wasn't a bullet that smashed this. Someone knocked all the jagged edges out, then maybe reached in to unlock the window. It was unlatched when I opened it."

"Is that how he got in? The guy who searched this place?"

"It would explain why the apartment door

wasn't forced. It also suggests that Phillip didn't invite his intruder in."

Logan was turning away from the window when Daisy placed a hand on his arm. "I'm sorry for tackling you. I overreacted."

The apology was unexpected. And it was undeserved. "Forget it. I should have checked the fire escape sooner. And you didn't overreact back at the cabin. You saved both our lives."

"Thanks." Her smile spread slowly. "I'm going to get better at this P.I. thing. You'll see." With that, she moved to the refrigerator, and opened the door. "I read that people hide all sorts of stuff in their freezers."

"Find anything?" Logan asked as he methodically checked drawers and cabinets.

"Fuzzy ice cream and moldy cheese." Stooping over, she surveyed the pots and canned goods scattered across the floor. "Phillip didn't cook much."

"Did he ever talk about sailing? Deep-sea fishing?"

"Phillip?" Glancing up, Daisy shook her head. "Never."

"This calendar." Logan pointed to the wall. "It's something a business mails out to advertise." He flipped pages. "And the business is a charter-boat place in the Bahamas."

Daisy picked her way through the mess to get a closer look.

"Were you going there on your honeymoon?" Logan asked.

She ran her finger along the ribbon of white sand in the picture. "We couldn't agree on a place to go. I wanted exotic. Phillip wanted practical."

"How exotic?"

"Oh, Greece, then Cairo, for starters," Daisy said with a laugh. "I've always had this dream of being able to touch a pyramid or walk up the steps of the Parthenon. Phillip suggested a week at the Waldorf here in town. I could go to the museum while he was at the office."

No wonder you needed a magic bed with that guy. The words were on the tip of his tongue. But he changed his mind about saying them aloud the moment he looked into her eyes. Instead, he said. "I stood in the center of the Roman Colosseum once. It was early afternoon, the sun was beating down, and for a moment I could have sworn I heard the roar of the crowd. I know I smelled blood." Suddenly he frowned. Where had that come from? He'd never told anyone about it before. He'd barely been able to admit it to himself.

Daisy laid a hand on his arm. "I knew it. I've always believed that ancient places, ancient things must have a power, a passion that lingers, that can draw you in and hold you."

Logan stared at her. She might have been speaking about herself, about the power that she seemed to have over him since he'd made love to her in that bed. He recalled the music he'd heard that had led him to the cabin. A power that could draw him in and hold him? No. He couldn't let himself believe in that. Couldn't let that happen. Jerking his arm free, he started toward the bedroom. "You said you could tell if he packed anything."

Daisy followed him to the doorway. The violence of the search was more evident here. The closet doors were open, but the clothes now covered the floor. Sheets had been torn from the bed, the mattress lay at an angle across the box spring, and every drawer had been dragged out and emptied.

As if reading her thoughts, Logan gave her shoulder a brief squeeze. "It's a good sign. If the searcher was getting angry, that means he wasn't finding what he was looking for."

Daisy picked her way through the debris, then suddenly bent to retrieve a pair of trousers from behind an overturned chair. "Phillip was wearing these at the office yesterday afternoon."

"You're sure?" Logan asked.

She lifted a jacket. "It's a new suit. He bought it for my aunt's funeral."

"That means he must have come back here to change. And pack?" They moved toward the suitcase together. It was empty.

"All right." Logan gave the room another quick scan. "We know he snuck out of the office. Otherwise, my operative would have spotted him leaving. So let's say he made a quick trip back here to change and pack, and he's interrupted. He hears the glass shatter." Moving back to the door, he glanced around the rest of the apartment. "He could have made it out the door before the intruder spotted him."

"So he's on the run. He's not our villain," Daisy said.

"Not so fast. He's running from someone or something. All it means is that he may not be our *only* villain."

Nudging the mattress more securely onto the bed, Daisy sat down. "Who is he running from? And why?"

Logan sat down next to her. "There are three great motivators. Greed, revenge and obsession. In this case I'm betting on greed. And the money trail leads back to Eddie Maplethorpe, your aunt's new will and the people who profit from it."

"My cousin Stevie and me."

"And Phillip, just as soon as he marries you."

"Then why is he on the run now? Why didn't he wait until after we're married?" Daisy asked.

"Something happened to change his plans. To make him panic. I'm guessing it was Eddie Maplethorpe's death. Or the fact that I suspected it might be murder. When I told him I didn't think Eddie's death was an accident, I saw the fear in his eyes."

"You're pretty sure there was something funny about the will, aren't you?"

"Maplethorpe turns up with it after your aunt's death, then disappears. Baldwin asks me to find this lawyer who drew up a will for one of Hanover Securities' clients. Soon after, Maplethorpe is the victim of a hit-and-run driver. I'd say it's a good bet that there's something funny about that will."

"But I recognized Aunt Angela's signature," Daisy said.

"I'm not saying your aunt didn't sign it," Logan said. "There are lots of ways to get a signature on a piece of paper." Rising, Logan began to pace. "What would have happened to the four million dollars if that will hadn't shown up?"

"It would have been held in trust at Hanover Securities for Stevie and me until we turned thirty."

"Why did your aunt leave half of her money to you? You're just her niece. Why not leave it all to her daughter?"

Daisy raised her shoulders and dropped them. "She loved me. I'm ten years older than Stevie. When my parents died, my uncle flew to the Caribbean to bring me back, and for eight years they raised me as their own daughter. They didn't even think they could have children until Stevie came along."

Logan thought for a minute. "So the only change in the new will was that you and Stevie inherited your legacies early."

"Right," Daisy said.

"What's your cousin doing with her share?"

"She's currently fighting with her father over it. He wants her to leave it at Hanover Securities until she's older. She wants to prove to him that she can invest it herself."

"So as a result of this new will, your uncle is losing a four-million-dollar account and Hanover Securities stands to lose at least your cousin's two million?"

Daisy frowned. "I hadn't thought of it that way. But you're right, I suppose."

"I'll have Ray check it out tomorrow. In the meantime, we'd better finish up here," Logan said as he looked around the room again. "We know that Phillip left the office early. The fact that he used the back entrance indicates he must have suspected that someone might follow him. Yet he must have thought that he had time enough to come back here, change, perhaps pack...and make some plans."

When his gaze came to rest on the phone sitting on the nightstand, Logan moved to the side of the bed and squatted. Beneath an upended drawer, he found a pencil and a blank notepad. Tossing them on the bed, he turned a phone book over and shook it. Nothing fell out. He reached for the phone. "Let's see who he called last."

"Look," Daisy said. "There's something on the notepad, an impression from whatever was written on the sheet on top." Turning the pencil on its side, she traced it lightly back and forth across the paper. "I saw Cary Grant do this in *North by Northwest*. Just a minute. There." She handed the notepad to Logan. "A four-digit number. Does it mean anything to you?"

"It might." Lifting the receiver, Logan pushed the redial button. When an airline-service representative answered, he settled himself on the bed next to Daisy. "I think we're in business."

Ten minutes later, they knew the number Daisy had shaded to life was the flight number of a plane leaving on Monday evening for Grand Cayman in the Bahamas. And Phillip Baldwin had booked a one-way ticket on it.

One ticket, one way. For a moment after he hung up the phone, neither one of them spoke.

Any satisfaction Logan might have felt was dimmed by his awareness of Daisy sitting next to him on the bed. She hadn't said a word since she'd handed him the notepad. He knew very well what she was feeling. Even if she wasn't in love with the guy, she'd trusted him. It was going to give him great pleasure to get his hands on Phillip Baldwin. Turning to Daisy, he searched for something to say.

"I wish you wouldn't," Daisy said.

"What?"

"Say *I told you so*. You did. Several times in fact. And you were right. Phillip is obviously in this right up to his neck. Go ahead. Gloat if you want."

"Things could be worse."

She turned to him then. "How? I agreed to marry a man who was probably just out to get my money. Then I find out that he might have had a hand in…arranging things so that I would get the money in the first place. Plus—" she waved a hand "—there's the matter of a hit-and-run. In which case, he might have used my car to kill a man—so in a pinch he could frame me for it! And now he's planning on making his getaway to the Bahamas. Have I left anything out?"

"Only the strong possibility that Phillip isn't in this alone."

"Great. There's more bad news to look forward to."

"Think of it this way. You could have gotten *him* into that magic bed instead of me. Then *he'd* be your soul mate."

Daisy stared at him, her eyes narrowing.

Slowly, she smiled. "You're teasing me, aren't you? You have the best deadpan expression. I wouldn't want to play poker with you." Leaning toward him, she gave him a quick kiss on the cheek. "And you're very sweet. Thanks."

"Thanks? For what?"

"Making me face the truth about Phillip. For trying to make me laugh instead of cry. For finding some kind of a clue in all this mess. You even suspected where he was going when you saw that calendar in the kitchen. Sherlock Holmes couldn't have done a better job. You're a genius!"

It was Logan's turn to stare. The sadness had disappeared from her eyes. It had been replaced by amusement just as he'd wanted it to be. But now he saw admiration, too. Only it was for someone who didn't exist.

Muttering an oath, Logan grabbed her shoulders and brought her face close to his. "Take a good look at me. I'm *not* a genius. I'm *not* Sherlock Holmes, James Bond or any of the other fictional heroes you conjure up in that fascinating mind of yours. And I'm certainly not sweet." In one swift move, he pulled her onto his lap and covered her mouth with his.

She would know who was kissing her this time. That was his driving thought as he ran his hands up her body and into her hair. Her skin was hot satin, her curls cool silk. Then her taste exploded into him, and he forgot everything else. The flavor was just as he'd remembered. Sweet and tart at the same time. Lemonade on a hot, summer day. He'd never been able to get enough of it when he'd been a child.

And her scent—wildflowers and spring rain. It didn't smell anything like the hot Texas land he'd grown up on. Still, it made him think of home.

And that was dangerous. The thought made its way into his mind. But he ignored it, shifting the angle of the kiss so that he could take more. In a moment, just a moment, this dreadful hunger would be appeased. It was his last thought before he lost himself in her.

There were so many reasons why she should push him away. In the space of a heartbeat, they streamed out of her mind. She could almost see them evaporate into steam. Just before she forgot everything but him. His mouth, so hard and hungry. His taste, dark and so very male. And his hands, demanding, unbearably arousing. One was fisted in her hair. The other swept over her in one claiming stroke, setting off wave after wave of liquid fire.

She was his.

He'd touched her before, kissed her before. But not like this. Not as though he intended to go on kissing her, touching her forever. And there was nothing, no one she wanted more. This was not her dream lover of the night. The gentleness was gone. Logan would take what he wanted, when he wanted. The pleasure of it, the power of it filled and delighted her. Gone was the fantasy. This was real. This man. These demands. No one had ever made her feel this way.

No one ever would. This was what she wanted. What she would always crave.

Curling her fingers into his sweater, she dragged him closer, determined to have more. Then, using her teeth and tongue, she took.

More. The word pounded in his brain as she wrapped herself around him and ran her hands over him. More. With an oath, he shifted her so that she lay beneath him on the bed. He'd been wanting her, hadn't been able to stop wanting her ever since he'd found her in that damn bed. So he would take her. Here. Now. Before the jagged need clawing through him ripped him apart. His hands moved to tear at the snap of her jeans.

On the table beside the bed, the phone began to ring. He could barely hear it above the pounding of her heart. Of his. It shrilled again, this time louder. On the third ring, Logan pulled away and stared down at her while he struggled for a breath. Her eyes were wide, clouded. Her lips, parted, moist, swollen from his kiss… He tore his eyes away so he could think. The phone.

"Have to…answer it." Levering himself off her, he drew her up so that she was sitting beside him. "Can you?"

When she nodded, he picked up the receiver. Later he would think about how his hand shook.

"Hello. Uncle Daniel? No, I'm here looking for Phillip. No, he's not. I don't know where… I got back this afternoon… Uncle Daniel, just listen for a second. Phillip didn't come with me to the Catskills. I haven't seen him since yesterday afternoon." For a moment she merely listened, then holding her hand over the receiver, Daisy whispered to Logan. "When Phillip left the office early yesterday, he told Uncle Daniel that we'd had a lovers' spat. He was going to go after me and try to get to the Catskills before the storm broke. That would explain why he came back here to pack— What?" Taking her hand off the receiver, Daisy spoke into the phone. "Say that again…the police… What did they want? Yes, I'll be there in the morning… Wait, don't hang—"

Letting out a frustrated breath, she handed the receiver to Logan. "He hung up. He's the most exasperating man. He *never* listens. He just plows ahead, full steam. You know, that's why I didn't have any suspicions about Aunt Angela's will. I figured she wanted to make a change, Uncle Daniel wasn't listening to her, and so she hired an attorney on her own."

"What did he say about the police?" Logan asked.

"They came to the house today asking about Eddie Maplethorpe. He had Uncle Daniel's home and office phone numbers in his wallet. The police said it was strictly routine, but they want to talk to Phillip and me too."

"If the police are asking about Maplethorpe, then they've turned up something that's making them suspicious about his death."

"They'll ask to see my car, won't they? What are we going to do?"

"Find Phillip," Logan said. "And get some answers."

"Phillip. I almost forgot. He told Uncle Daniel

he was coming after me. But he never made it. What if he had an accident? What if he's—"

Logan gripped Daisy's shoulders. "Take it easy. If he ever intended to follow you, I think he changed his mind after he got back here and almost ran into his intruder. Or maybe he did follow you. Maybe he was the one who shot at us this morning. Did you ever think of that?"

Daisy stared at Logan. "But why would he? Especially if he's running away from someone too." She shook her head. "It doesn't make any sense. None of it makes any sense."

"No, it doesn't."

Even as he said the words, she saw the change in his eyes, and she knew he wasn't just talking about Phillip's disappearance anymore. He was talking about them, about what they'd been doing, what they'd be doing right now if the phone hadn't interrupted. Beneath the palm of her hand, the mattress was still warm. A quick thrill of panicked excitement whipped through her. If he moved now, if he reached out and touched her, would she stop him? Would he let her stop him?

"We can't," Daisy said as she jumped up. "It's that bed. It's bewitched us."

"It has nothing to do with that damn bed."

"How else do you account for it? If we'd met under other circumstances, we wouldn't have even looked at each other."

"We both took a good long look in that elevator."

Suddenly she recalled exactly what she felt when she'd first seen him—that strange shock of recognition. "Okay, you've got a point. But whatever we saw, whatever we felt, we would never have acted on it. Admit it. We're too different." Daisy ticked off the points on her fingers. "You're an adventurer. The only adventures I have are in the books I read. You're a loner. I have a family who depends on me. We have absolutely nothing in common. None of this would be going on if we hadn't spent the night in that bed together."

Logan studied her for a moment, once again thoroughly intrigued by the way her mind worked. The problem was that there was always a thin thread of logic mixed in with everything she said. It fascinated him at the same time that it annoyed the hell out of him. Absolutely everything she said was true. They *were* different. They were all wrong for each other. And they couldn't possibly have a future.

A *future*? Was that what he was thinking of having with Daisy Hanover?

"This has got to stop," Daisy said. "Look at us. We're supposed to be looking for Phillip. Instead, the police are looking for me, or they will be if I don't show up at the house tomorrow. Once they see my car and that scrap of cloth with the button, they'll arrest me for running down Eddie Maplethorpe. And instead of doing anything about it, we almost..." She backed up one quick step. "We almost made love on *Phillip's* bed!"

Logan rose, but he didn't touch her. He didn't trust himself to touch her. "Try this for an explanation. I want you, and you want me. The next time we won't *almost* make love. We will. And it will have nothing to do with that damn bed, magic or not. It will just be me and you." He walked toward the door. "C'mon."

"Where?" she asked as she hurried after him.

"To find Phillip."

They were almost there when she heard the scrape of metal against metal. Beyond Logan's shoulder, Daisy saw the doorknob turning. Then Logan whirled, covering her mouth with his hand as he pressed her against the wall. "Don't argue," he whispered. "Take the fire escape to the upstairs apartment. Phone the police."

The door burst open, and whacked loudly against a wall. Logan took time to give Daisy one good shove toward the kitchen before he turned to find a huge hulk of a man bearing down on him. He had just time enough to brace himself before two hundred and fifty pounds of muscle and bulk slammed into him. Together they flew against the couch, toppling it over. Springs snapped and a lamp crashed against the wall as they rolled across the floor.

Before Logan could get to his feet, the big man was on him, grabbing his throat and cutting off his air. Freeing his arm, Logan aimed his fist at the man's windpipe. The fingers around his neck tightened. His vision grayed, and he saw a blur of motion. Daisy launching herself onto the thug's back, pounding his head with her fists. Fear and fury fused within him as the mountain roared, surged to his feet and spun wildly in a circle. Daisy flew off and dropped to the floor.

Rolling into a crouched position, Logan aimed low and torpedoed himself into the mountain. It was like trying to tackle the Great Wall of China. Pain sang through every bone as he was slammed back against a wall. Using it for leverage, he aimed a two-footed kick at the man's face and heard the satisfying crunch of bone just before he fell flat on his back and the wind left his body.

Struggling for a breath, Logan caught a glimpse of Daisy flying forward again, a table leg cocked at the ready. She managed to whack the big man once in the head before he flung out an arm and sent her rolling across the floor. Then the hulk surged to his feet and lunged for the door.

Rolling to his knees, Logan reached for a foot and felt it slip out of his grasp. By the time he made it into the hallway, the door to the stairwell had swung shut. He could hear the thunder of footsteps. He took two running steps in pursuit before he swore and turned back.

Daisy was on her knees, leaning against a wall and struggling for air. Dropping down beside her, Logan grabbed her shoulders. "Are you all right?"

"He's going to have...a bad headache," she managed to say.

He wanted to throttle her. He settled for pulling her close and holding her tight as images raced through his mind. Daisy riding on the man's back, sailing through the air, falling to the floor. Running a hand up her back and into her hair, he drew her closer. She didn't resist, but neither did she cling.

Fearless. That's what she'd been. The realization had the terror building in him anew. Drawing her away, he tightened his grip on her shoulders. "Stupid!" He gave her a shake. "I told you to get out."

"I don't desert…a partner," she said.

The feelings swamped him then. He wasn't even sure what they were. Wasn't sure he wanted to know. Pulling her against him, he gave her a desperate kiss, then drew her even closer and buried his face in her hair.

"Logan, I—"

"Shut up." He was trembling. "You scared me."

"Me, too," she said, wrapping her arms around him and holding him tight.

For a moment, he gave in to the need to go on holding her. For just a minute, he promised himself as one minute stretched into two. As the pulse of her heartbeat slowed against him, he felt his own grow steadier too. Only then did some of his fear begin to ease.

This was different from when he'd held her moments before on the bed. He felt none of that turbulent passion, the almost brutal desire. Yet he wanted to go on holding her… Abruptly, he drew away.

Daisy met his eyes. "If you're sure it's all right for me to talk, I have a question."

The laugh burst from him before he could prevent it, and as he rested his forehead briefly against hers, he felt the rest of his tension stream away. "Why am I not surprised?"

"Who was that sumo wrestler, and what did he want?"

Logan rose, drawing her with him. "That's two questions."

"I have a lot more."

Keeping his arm around her, Logan urged her toward the door. "So do I, Daze. So do I. What do you say we find us some answers?"

7

Using a towel to wipe steam off the bathroom mirror, Daisy checked her reflection. She *looked* just like the old Daisy.

The problem was she didn't *feel* like the old Daisy. Every single bone in her body ached. Twisting, she checked the bruise that was forming on her shoulder, then gingerly pressed her fingers to the bump on the back of her head. She felt more like Xena, the Warrior Princess. On a bad day.

The corners of her mouth twitched. The truth was, she was enjoying working with Logan. Did that mean she was turning into a masochist?

"No," she said as the frightening realization struck her. "It means I'm turning into my father!"

She waited then, holding her breath for one of the voices in her head to disagree.

No one said a word.

It was a serious situation indeed when both sides of her nature were in agreement. With a sigh, Daisy sank onto the edge of the bathtub and stared straight ahead.

Andrew Hanover had given up everything to run away with his true love. Even as the thought slipped into her mind, Daisy shot to her feet.

No! It was that bed! Instead of a Celtic inscription on the headboard, there should have been a warning in bright, blinking neon letters: *Do not get into this bed with the wrong man!*

Pressing her hand against her stomach, Daisy took a deep breath and waited for the bubble of panic to subside. She couldn't possibly be falling in love with Logan. It was just lust.

Daisy snatched her clothes, and quickly pulled them on. There was a big difference between lust and love.

What was it?

That was the question.

She stared at her reflection in the mirror again. She'd never really known about lust until she met Logan. And all she knew about love was what she'd read in books or seen in movies. Rhett and Scarlett. Rick and Elsa from Casablanca. Romeo and Juliet.

Not one happy ending in the bunch! And she'd believed a magic bed would give her one?

How could she be sure she was falling in love with Logan? She wasn't even sure who he was. What she needed was time. Time to get to know him better. Time to decide what to do.

And she wasn't sure how much she had. Ray and Logan had been in his office working for over two hours trying to locate Phillip. They'd called and faxed pictures of Phillip to their contacts on newspapers, hospitals, even a few hotels. Any minute now, they could call it a day.

That would leave her alone with Logan.

And there was only one bed.

Opening the bathroom door a crack, Daisy

studied the sofa bed. It might not have any magic power, but she could tell by looking that it would be small when it was pulled out. She could imagine quite clearly what it would be like to lie on that bed with Logan and…

Quickly, Daisy shut the bathroom door and rested her head against it. Was she ever going to be able to look at a bed again without imagining herself on it with Logan Campbell? Was she ever going to be able to think about Logan Campbell without imagining what it would be like to make love with him again?

She had to get a grip. She had to follow the number-one rule of a good P.I. and be objective. The only solution was to look at Logan as a research project. Maybe if she did that, she could conquer this lust thing and make an intelligent, informed decision.

Feeling more confident, Daisy opened the door and stepped into the room.

"Anywhere you want, sugar, but I'll have to get back to you on the when."

Daisy stopped in her tracks. It was Logan's voice coming from the other room. But she'd never heard him use that sexy, tempting tone before.

"I won't have much time until I track down this Phillip Baldwin. I'll have Ray fax you a picture now. Keep an eye out, will you?"

"Sure thing, Logan. Remember, I miss you."

Daisy's fingers curled into claws. She'd taken one step toward the door to the office before she realized that the soft, purry voice was coming from the speakerphone.

Sure thing, Logan!

Whirling, she headed toward the small table where she'd laid out the sandwich supplies earlier. Grabbing a stack of bread slices, Daisy dealt them out like playing cards. Obviously, Logan Campbell knew how to push all the right buttons when it came to women. Well, Daisy wasn't the type to fall for that. With a knife, she slathered mustard on each slice, then slapped on ham and cheese.

Whatever she discovered about him, one thing she knew. She and Logan Campbell were all wrong for each other. It was just another example to prove her point. He'd never talked to her in that particular tone. It was probably one he reserved exclusively for his *women friends*.

Gripping the knife handle firmly, Daisy whacked the first sandwich in half.

"I'd hate to run into you in a dark alley."

Daisy turned abruptly and found Ray observing her from the doorway. She managed a smile. The man had been at the office fifteen minutes after Logan had called him, and he'd been working tirelessly ever since. "I avoid dark alleys," she said. "I was just taking out my frustration on some ham and swiss. Want one?"

"Sure," Ray said, moving to take the one she offered. "You know, detective work seems slow and tedious, but it does get results. Absolutely every contact we have in Manhattan is on the lookout for Phillip."

It occurred to her then that she hadn't been thinking of Phillip. She'd been too busy being jealous of all the other women in Logan Campbell's life.

"What if he's not in Manhattan?" she asked.

Ray shrugged. "Logan will find him. He'll discover some little thing that will point the way. With Eddie Maplethorpe it was a pack of matches in his desk drawer. It advertised a restaurant in the town we tracked him to."

"You've been working for Logan for a long time?" Daisy asked.

"Ever since I got out of jail on parole," Ray said. When Daisy's eyes widened, he grinned at her. "I got sent up for computer fraud when I was seventeen. It was a nice white-collar federal facility, but it was still jail. When I got out, Logan took a chance on me, and I'm still here."

"I can't get rid of him," Logan said as he entered the room. "I thought I told you to hit the road."

"I needed fuel," Ray said. Winking at Daisy, he grabbed another sandwich and made his way out. "I'll be back at 8:00 a.m. Sleep tight, you two."

The words hung in the air for several beats after the outer door closed behind Ray. Daisy picked up the knife and busied herself slicing the rest of the sandwiches. When she glanced up, Logan was still in the doorway leaning against the jamb. He looked tired. She felt an almost overwhelming urge to go to him, slip her arms around him and hold him. Just for a moment. It wasn't lust she was feeling.

Still, lust or not, she knew exactly where it would lead. Desperately, Daisy tried to remember her plan. She was going to learn more about Logan Campbell. "Are you hungry? Or do you want more coffee?"

"No, we both need some sleep. The sofa pulls out into a—"

The instant Logan moved forward, Daisy stepped into his path, putting both hands out to stop him. "No—"

"Daisy—"

"Don't interrupt. I have to say this. And I will. I figured it out in the shower. I can't...I mean, we can't..."

But Logan knew they could. All he had to do was reach out, draw her to him. Kiss her. She knew it too. It was right there in her eyes. She wanted. He wanted.

It should have been easy. He should have just been able to reach out and start what they both wanted. It should have been so simple. It wasn't.

It was the damnedest thing. Logan had to clench his hands into fists to keep them at his sides. The battle he was waging wasn't with her. It was with himself. And it was a first. He wasn't sure if it was a victory when he stepped back from her. He had to put a great deal of effort into the smile. "Let me guess. You're going to play hard to get."

Daisy blinked, then narrowed her eyes. "It's not a matter of playing hard to get. It's a matter of getting to know one another—and I don't see what's so funny!"

"I'm not laughing."

"Your eyes are. You were serious enough when you said you wanted me to know who it was the next time we made love. And I agree, one hundred percent. So I'd like to get to know you better before I...before you..."

"Before *we* jump onto another bed."

Lifting her chin, Daisy met his eyes. "*If* we ever jump—"

Logan took a step toward her. It was enough to have their bodies almost brushing again. "*When* we make love again, I don't much care where we do it. We could even try it standing up, if you'd like." Lifting his wrist, he glanced at his watch. "As far as time goes, we both know it's running out."

"Oh, and when it does? What then?" She poked a finger into his chest. "I'm not some woman who's so overwhelmed by your charm that you just have to push a button and I'll say, 'Sure thing.' When I'm ready to make love to you—if I'm ready—I'll...I'll...whistle!"

Logan's grin blossomed slowly into a laugh that filled the small room. "I'll be waiting. In the meantime, you can have the sofa all to yourself." Turning, he moved to the door, then looked back.

"What?" Daisy asked.

"Just checking to see if you'd puckered up yet." He managed to shut the door before a ham sandwich splatted against it.

SHE'D SLEPT like a rock. And he hadn't. Leaning against the car, Logan began filling it with gas as he watched Daisy walk into the convenience store. He'd found himself checking on her several times during the night. By his third visit, he'd begun to feel like some knight of old keeping watch over his lady.

He hadn't liked the analogy one damn bit. Knights and ladies operated in a world of magic and spells. And he didn't believe in them.

Through the window of the store, he could see her loading disposable cups onto a paper tray, laughing at something the cashier said to her. She was the strangest mixture, he thought as she stepped through the door and walked toward him. Different from any woman he'd ever known. On the one hand, she was too cautious to convert the sofa in his office into a bed that would sleep two, and on the other, she was too fearless to run from that hulk who'd attacked them at Phillip's apartment.

Daisy Hanover was completely incomprehensible. And this morning she was annoying the hell out of him. Frowning, he replaced his gas cap and hung up the hose. She was treating him like some kind of research project, hounding him with questions. She'd even borrowed a notebook from him to scribble down his answers.

He'd diverted her temporarily when he'd explained the "role" he'd be playing when they arrived at her family's home. She was to introduce him to her uncle and cousin as Jack Whitmore, her newly hired assistant at the bookstore.

In answer to her barrage of questions, he'd explained that the number-two rule of a good P.I. was never to introduce yourself as a private investigator unless you absolutely had to.

"I paid for the gas," she said as she circled

around the front of the car and climbed in. When he joined her, she offered him one of the cups. "I didn't know how 'Jack' likes his coffee, so I brought cream and sugar."

"Black's fine," Logan said as he set the coffee on the dash and nosed the car out onto the highway.

"And how do you take your coffee when you're Logan Campbell?" Daisy asked.

"Black's fine for him too. Let me know when I should turn."

"It's a ways yet. Just before we get to the village sign." Daisy took a sip of her coffee, then turned so she could study Logan's profile. "So when you change into these characters, you still keep the same likes and dislikes?"

"It makes it simpler," Logan said.

"So basically you're still Logan Campbell. It's just the clothes that have changed?"

"You could say that."

Daisy took another sip. The man sitting behind the wheel of the car was a sharp right turn away from the Logan Campbell she'd first met in the elevator. She could see her James Bond man as the Ninja warrior who'd double-kicked the thug in Phillip's apartment last night.

But the man in the driver's seat next to her was different. Her gaze flicked over the button-down collar, the tweed jacket and the faded jeans. It was partly the clothes, but the glasses and the narrow mustache certainly added to the effect. But the transformation went a lot deeper. His walk was a little slower, his gestures more precise. Even his speech pattern had changed. It was slower, more in keeping with his academic background. Jack Whitmore was a part-time grad student.

"It's more than the outfit. Everything about you has changed. If you'd walked into my bookstore and applied for a job, I think I would have hired you."

Logan flashed her a quick grin. "You can bet on it, sugar."

"I wouldn't hire anyone who called me sugar."

"In that case, I apologize, Ms. Hanover."

"It's got to be confusing going back and forth. Kind of like having a split personality. Do you ever forget and start acting like James Bond when you're supposed to be someone else?"

"I told you before. I'm *not* James Bond."

Daisy waved a hand. "Right. But you're not this Jack Whitmore either. I'm just trying to figure out who you are."

"Today, I'm Jack Whitmore. Try to remember that when you introduce me to your uncle. Is this the turn?"

Daisy glanced at the road. "Go right. And then left between the stone posts." The moment he swerved into the driveway, Daisy said, "I understand why you don't want me to introduce you as Logan Campbell. But I've been thinking maybe we should tell Uncle Daniel everything we know. He didn't have anything to do with Aunt Angela's will, so he had no reason to kill Eddie Maplethorpe."

Logan glanced at her. "Go ahead. Pretend I'm

your uncle. Give me an outline of what you suspect so far."

"A sniper tried to kill you or maybe both of us at the cabin."

"Or maybe the sniper was after Phillip since Baldwin told your uncle that he was going there when he left the office."

Daisy frowned. "Okay, so we don't know who the sniper was after for sure. But we could at least tell Uncle Daniel that Phillip's apartment has been ransacked, and that when we went there looking for Phillip, we were attacked by someone who looked like a professional wrestler."

"And we're not sure whether the wrestler was after us or Phillip either," Logan added. "Are you going to tell him that we think your aunt's will might have been a fake, and that Eddie Maplethorpe might have been killed because of his involvement in that little scam?"

"I hadn't thought of that. He'll go ballistic," Daisy said. "Stevie's birthday is tomorrow. As executor of my aunt's will, he could use it as an excuse not to give her the money. She'll have a fit." Daisy could see bright neon letters blinking in front of her eyes: *Disaster!* "Okay. You win. Forget I even suggested telling him anything."

"The number-three rule of a good P.I. is never to give out more information that you absolutely have to," Logan said with a smile. "Let's just see what we can find out from your uncle and your cousin."

As the car swept around the last curve of the driveway and the house came into view, Daisy let her gaze return to Logan. No, Jack Whitmore, she reminded herself. She could picture him in her shop right now. It was a little harder to picture Logan there.

Suddenly, she realized that she felt more comfortable with Jack. He didn't look so secretive, so dangerous. It would probably be different going to bed with Jack, too.

The moment Daisy realized the direction her thoughts had taken was the exact moment that Logan braked to a stop and turned to meet her eyes.

"What?" he asked. Then his eyes narrowed.

Daisy felt the heat rise to her face as she watched Logan's lips curve into a wide grin.

"Whatever it is, hold on to that thought, Daze," he said as he gave her a quick, hard kiss.

In the time it took him to climb out and circle the car to open her door, Daisy drew in a deep steadying breath. She was definitely attracted to Jack Whitmore.

Oh, it might not be the same kind of attraction she felt for Logan, but it was there just the same.

Did that make her promiscuous? she wondered.

This was one complication the Bond girls had never run into. James was never anyone but James.

She'd barely stepped out of the car when Uncle Daniel stormed onto the front porch.

"It's high time you two got here." Then he gave Logan a second look. "You're not Phillip."

It was an accusation that had Daisy and Logan both moving forward. Logan extended his hand. "I'm Jack Whitmore, sir. Your niece's new assistant at the bookstore."

"New assistant?" Frowning, Daniel turned to Daisy. "You sure you can afford to hire one?"

"Absolutely," Daisy said, taking her uncle's arm and urging him back into the house. "Women buy sixty percent of the mass-market paperbacks each year. With Jack working in the store, I expect sales to soar."

"Hmm," Daniel said, giving Logan an assessing glance before he turned back to Daisy. "Phillip said the two of you'd had a little misunderstanding. Did you call off the wedding?"

"No. I told you on the phone. I don't know where Phillip is. He never made it to the Catskills. He's not at his apartment. I was hoping you'd heard from him by now."

Daniel frowned. "I haven't heard from him since he went hightailing it out of the office on Friday afternoon. I never did understand why the two of you wanted to go off to the Catskills this weekend anyway. The wedding is in two weeks. Time enough to take a honeymoon then. Told Phillip so myself. That's the way we did it in my day."

"I'm worried," Daisy said. "I even checked with the state police. They don't have a report on him. Can you think of anywhere he could have gone?"

Eyes narrowed, Daniel studied Daisy. "You're really worried about him?"

Daisy nodded.

"My guess is he got waylaid by that storm.

Could be he went on to the cabin once the roads were cleared. Why don't you call and see?"

"There's no phone," Daisy said.

"Then you'll just have to wait." Taking one of her hands, he patted it. "Tell you what. If he doesn't show up for work tomorrow, that's when I'll start to worry. He's about to take a long walk down the aisle. That's a big step for a man. Could be he needs a little time to himself."

Glancing at his watch, he said, "Why don't you give Stevie a call? She spent the night at the Gibsons'. Delores will have brunch ready in an hour. Since I came home this weekend to be with my family, it'd be nice if they cared enough to show up." Then, turning to Logan, he said, "Don't suppose you play chess?"

"As a matter of fact, I do," Logan said.

"C'mon then. We have time for a game before we eat." Turning on his heel, Daniel led the way down a long hallway.

THIRTY MINUTES LATER, Daisy left the two men alone in her uncle's library. Not that they would miss her. They were equally matched, at chess as well as at pumping each other for information. Even in that short amount of time, Logan had gotten a brief rundown on the kind of investing Hanover Securities was involved in, including Phillip's place in the firm. And Uncle Daniel now knew more than Daisy ever cared to about Jack Whitmore.

He was taking graduate courses in archaeology! It was when she'd caught herself envisioning how Logan would look wearing Indiana

Jones's fedora that she'd decided she had to do something. Anything.

Stopping in the hallway, she picked up the phone and tried the Gibsons—where Stevie had spent the night. There'd been no answer earlier. When the answering machine picked up, she left another message.

A quick glance in the kitchen confirmed her suspicion that Delores wasn't in need of any help. Stuffing her hands in her pockets, Daisy wandered up the stairs to her room. She was feeling bored and superfluous. The downside of leading an adventurous life, she supposed.

Moving toward the windows, she looked out at the backyard. A sudden gust of wind sent snow swirling off the roof, and the sun glinted off the flakes as they showered to the ground. What did a Bond girl do when James didn't need her? she wondered.

A little sleuthing on her own. Daisy was willing to bet on it. Tapping her fingers against the window ledge, she thought hard. What if Uncle Daniel was right and Phillip had followed her all the way to the cabin, and they'd just missed each other? He would have had to walk in through the woods. She doubted they had cleared the driveway yet. And he would have seen her car, so he would have known she'd been there. Was he waiting for her?

Or was he too in hiding from whoever it was who'd shot at them and busted into Phillip's apartment? And where would Phillip hide? Snow fell in a sudden shower off the eaves of the garage. Suddenly her gaze narrowed.

She was looking out the window at the perfect hiding place. There was a small apartment over the garage. Originally, it had been built as living quarters for a chauffeur, but Daniel had never used one and so the space had remained unoccupied. And Phillip had known about the apartment. Daniel had even offered it to him. He'd often stayed over to work weekends during Aunt Angela's illness.

Quickly, she moved to the dresser and pulled out a sweater. She had the drawer nearly shut when she saw it. A square white envelope with her name and address typed neatly. She'd never seen it before.

Curiosity mixed with fear as she lifted the envelope and studied the date on the postmark. Two weeks ago. Carefully, she pulled out a single folded sheet and opened it. Words and letters cut from a newspaper read:

I want a cut of your two million, or I'll reveal that your aunt's will was a fake.

There was no signature. But it didn't need one, Daisy thought as she slid the message back into the envelope. Her mind was racing as she backed slowly to the bed and sank onto it. Who had put the note there? And why?

There were only so many people who could have hidden it in her drawer. Besides her family, there was just Phillip. But why was someone trying to frame her for Eddie Maplethorpe's murder? Who would profit from that?

Not Phillip, certainly. She read the message

through again and tried to think. But it didn't make any sense. Logan had told her at the cabin that she was going to be the prime suspect once they turned over her car to the police. But it really hadn't sunk in until now. She pressed a hand to her temple.

One thing was sure. She wasn't going to stand idly by and let someone frame her for murder. She stuffed the letter into the pocket of her jeans and stood up. And she wasn't going to let the fear that had settled in an icy ball in her stomach stop her from searching that apartment over the garage. Heaven knew what she was going to find there.

Quickly, Daisy made her way down the stairs. Silence reigned in the library. And Delores was on the phone. Waving to the cook as she hurried through the kitchen, Daisy grabbed keys off the peg and ran across the breezeway to the garage.

Once inside, she stopped and listened. Nothing. The air was cold and smelled of gas. A sudden fall of snow outside made Daisy jump. Pressing her hand against her heart, she waited a minute for it to slow. Then she started up the stairs. Every little creak seemed to explode into the silence. At the top, she inserted the key, turned the knob and pushed the door open. The room was empty and dark. But it was warmer than the garage. Moving to a window, she drew the curtains aside. No one had lived in it for as long as she could remember. The linoleum was cracked, the walls cried out for paint and the furniture was from the same period as the stuff in Logan's office.

Just the thought of Logan gave her confidence. He'd be looking for clues. Something. Anything. She began her search by opening cupboards. There were a few pots and pans, some dishes, no food. The refrigerator was unplugged, its door ajar. A teakettle sat on a burner, empty and cold.

A sudden noise made her whirl. Had it been more falling snow? Someone on the stairs? She listened hard. The sound wasn't repeated. Her gaze swept the room, and she noticed the door to the bedroom was closed.

Quietly, Daisy walked toward it, trying to ignore the butterflies whipping around in her stomach. Maybe this sleuthing alone hadn't been such a good idea. It was much easier being brave when she had Logan for backup.

Taking a deep breath, she gripped the handle and pushed. The room was empty, but the blanket on the bed was mussed. Moving quickly around it, she entered the bathroom.

Nothing. It wasn't until then that she realized she'd stopped breathing. When she drew in air, she smelled it—Phillip's cologne. Whirling again, she expected to find him standing right behind her.

He wasn't. Then she spotted the towel. Lifting it, she breathed in again. It was Phillip's scent all right. And the towel was still damp. She checked the medicine cabinet above the sink. Empty. She glanced at the latch on the window above the sink. Locked.

Slowly, she walked back into the bedroom.

There were two places she hadn't looked—under the bed and inside the closet.

Taking another deep breath, she tried a different approach. "Phillip, are you in here?"

Silence. He'd answer her if he were here, wouldn't he?

There was only one way to make sure.

The bed first. It was definitely mussed, as if someone had slept on it. And if he'd heard her coming up the stairs, the closest place to hide was… Dropping to her knees, she took a quick look under the bed.

Dust bunnies.

Rising, she took one step toward the closet before her courage ran out.

"Who in the world do you think you are?" whispered the practical side of her. "Xena, the Warrior Princess? Go get Logan."

If she went to get Logan, she thought, Phillip might run away. *If* he was here. All she'd smelled was cologne. Besides, Phillip wasn't going to hurt her.

She took another step and then a third. It was a scene straight out of every horror movie she'd ever watched. Each step brought her closer to the closet door, the knob. As she reached for it, she pressed her free hand against her heart to keep it from pounding right out of her chest.

There wasn't a monster behind the door. It there was anyone there, it would be Phillip.

And if he was trying to frame her for Eddie Maplethorpe's death, he was going to explain why.

She twisted the knob and jerked it open.

Empty. She let out the breath she was holding. Then a sudden noise shot her heart straight up to her throat. This time she recognized the sound. Someone was climbing the stairs. Logan? She dashed for the apartment door, reaching for the handle, yanking it open.

She and the man on the other side of it both jumped.

"Mark!"

"Daisy, I didn't mean to startle you."

"I just didn't expect...I thought...what are you doing here?"

"I'm supposed to tutor Stevie today. Delores says she's still at the Gibsons', and that you were out here." He glanced past her into the room. "Look, Daisy," he said abruptly. "There's something I need to discuss with you. Do you mind if we talk here? I don't want your uncle to hear. Stevie either, if she happens to come home."

Stepping aside so that he could enter, Daisy said, "What is it?"

"Do you know for a fact that Stevie stayed at the Gibsons' last night?"

"That's what she told her father. What are you suggesting?"

"I'm worried about her. I..." Stuffing his hands in his pockets, Mark moved out to the kitchen, then turned. "For the past few weeks, she's been distracted when I'm tutoring her."

"*Distracted?*" Daisy smiled. "That's a nice way of putting it. Since her mother's death, she's cut off her hair, dyed it, started wearing leather and threatened to pierce her nose. I can think of other ways to describe Stevie besides *distracted*.

I'm hoping that when her father finally turns over her inheritance check to her tomorrow, she'll become less so."

Frowning, Mark began to pace. "It's more than the hair and the clothes. And more than the ongoing battle she's had with her father about the money. Lately, she's been talking about doing something to really prove something to her family. And…"

"What are you trying to tell me, Mark?"

"I don't have any proof. It's just a feeling. That's why I haven't come to you sooner. I've been very worried ever since she called and canceled our tutoring session on Friday. She said she had a doctor's appointment in the city. Afterward, I got worried about her because of the storm. But when I called the house, Delores claimed Stevie hadn't gone into the city. She was at a friend's house." Pausing, he faced Daisy. "There isn't any easy way to say this. I think she may be seeing someone."

"Stevie?" Daisy's first impulse was to tell him he was crazy. Then she recalled her cousin's words that day when they'd been looking at the Web site. Hadn't Stevie threatened to do something more shocking than pierce her nose?

"I don't want to upset you. And I could be wrong," Mark said.

"I'm sure you are. I think I'd have noticed. But I appreciate your concern. You've been very good to this family."

Mark smiled then, relaxing for the first time since he'd stepped into the apartment. "Stevie means a lot to me. You all do. When I was working here during your aunt's illness, well, I began to think of you as a kind of second family." Turning, he glanced into the bedroom. "What is this place anyway?"

"The people who built the house had a chauffeur."

"Has anyone been using it lately?" Mark asked, moving to the bed.

"Not since I've been living here."

Bending down, Mark lifted something from the folds of the blanket that lay half on and half off the bare mattress. Daisy recognized it immediately. It was an earring. And it belonged to Stevie. She stared at it.

"Am I interrupting something?"

Daisy whirled to face Logan in the doorway. The coolness of his tone contrasted sharply with the heat in his eyes. She felt singed. Swallowing, she said, "Mark, this is Jack Whitmore, my new assistant at the bookstore. Mark tutors Stevie in math."

"And I was just returning her earring." Giving it to Daisy, he shook Logan's hand.

"Daniel spotted you coming up here through the window and I think he has his sights set on a new victim. He wants to know if you have time for a game of chess."

"Absolutely, if it means an invitation to one of Delores's brunches."

When Daisy moved to follow Mark, Logan took her arm. "Mark, could you tell Daniel we'll be down in a few minutes? I'm going to take a look at this apartment as long as I'm here. I'm hoping to find something close to the bookstore."

"Sure thing." The moment Mark reached the bottom of the stairs, Logan closed the door and turned to Daisy. "Don't ever sneak off like that again."

If she'd felt singed before, the heat in his eyes was enough to burn her now. She lifted her chin. "I just had this idea that Phillip might be hiding out here. And I think he was." She led the way into the bedroom. "I smelled his cologne on a towel in the bathroom."

Logan stared at her. "You thought he was in this apartment and you came up here by yourself?"

"You were playing chess. Besides, I can handle Phillip."

Moving forward, he gripped her shoulders. "Maybe you could handle the Phillip you thought you knew. But he's not that man, Daze. When are you going to realize that?"

"I do. At least, I'm trying. But—"

"No *buts!* What if he was here but he wasn't alone? What if you'd run into that goon who barged into his apartment? Do you think anyone would have heard you scream?"

"All right." Daisy swallowed the tight ball of fear that had risen to her throat. "You've made your point."

"Then I have your word that from now on you won't go off on your own?"

Daisy's eyebrows lifted. "As long as it works both ways, and I get to come with you wherever you go."

Logan sighed. "Daze, I—"

"I'd be much more likely to remember not to go off by myself if I thought that I was a full partner in this investigation."

"I told you, I don't work with a partner." He paused, then, "You're sure Phillip was here?"

"Definitely. I could smell him in the bathroom. And the bed was mussed." Moving toward it, she lifted the blanket, and as she did, the earring she was holding dropped to the floor. She picked it up.

"There are footprints leading from the garage to the woods."

"Great." Daisy sank onto the bed. "You know, the downside of this P.I. business is that you actually find things out. Mark thinks Stevie is involved with someone."

He glanced back at her. "Does he know who?"

"No, he didn't have a name." She glanced down at her hands. She held the bedcover in one hand, the earring in the other. "But Phillip's been here. And Stevie's been here too. Mark found her earring on the bed. I can't believe that she'd... Not Stevie."

Logan went to her then, sat down beside her and lifted her onto his lap. Saying nothing, he stroked her hair.

It was so easy for Daisy to settle her head against his shoulder. "Go ahead. You can say it."

"What?"

"I told you so. You've been warning me all

along that family can betray you. I just can't believe..."

Logan still said nothing. He could say nothing to her to make this particular pain go away. He merely continued stroking her hair. And as he did, he felt his own fear begin to ease. It had sunk its jagged teeth in his gut the moment he'd realized that she wasn't in the house. And it hadn't helped one bit to find her talking to a stranger or to think of her alone in this apartment looking for Phillip. He ran his hand down the length of her back. She felt so soft, so fragile in his arms. And she felt right. She shouldn't, but she did.

"I simply don't believe it." She raised her head then.

Logan's eyes narrowed, but he managed to keep his voice calm. "What don't you believe? That Phillip could be sleeping with your cousin? How long are you going to insist on seeing him through rose-colored glasses?"

"I don't. I'm not saying that I don't believe Phillip might have tried to seduce Stevie, although it is a little difficult to figure out how he managed to fit it into his schedule. What I don't believe is that Stevie would get involved with Phillip. She just wouldn't do that to me. There must be some other way that her earring got in this bed."

"Phillip could have planted it."

Daisy thought about it for a minute, and her smile spread slowly. "I can see why they pay you the big bucks. Phillip *must* have planted it.

Just as he planted the blackmail letter in my dresser drawer."

"Blackmail letter?"

"Here." Shifting slightly, Daisy pulled it out.

Logan read the note quickly, then carefully slipped it back into the envelope. "Let's take it from the top. Phillip arranges for Maplethorpe to draw up a fake will so that he can marry an heiress who has the bonus of being the equivalent of the boss's daughter. Then he decides to get rid of Maplethorpe—maybe the guy got greedy and wanted a bigger cut. Then I show up, suspecting that old Eddie's been murdered, and he panics and decides to frame you for the murder."

For a moment neither of them spoke.

Finally Logan said, "I could drive a truck through the holes in that theory."

"Me, too. If I end up in jail, someone's bound to wonder about the will. Otherwise, what's my motive for running down Mr. Maplethorpe? And if the will is proved to be a fake, Phillip can't marry the heiress, unless seducing Stevie is his backup plan." Daisy frowned. "I don't think I like the way this theory is headed."

"Me, neither. Even if he does manage to get Stevie to marry him, chances are she won't be an heiress either, at least until she's thirty, because it's bound to come out at your murder trial that the will is a fake."

"So we're right back where we started?" asked Daisy.

"Unless I've been wrong about the motive. What if it isn't money that Phillip is after, but revenge? What if he's simply out to destroy you and your family?"

"But why?"

"I've got Ray digging a little deeper into Phillip's background, and he's running a check on everyone else who had access to your car and the house. I'm going to add your friend Mark to the list."

"Mark?" Daisy asked.

"Yeah. What do you know about him?"

"He's a private duty nurse who saved my sanity during the last few months before my aunt died. Uncle Daniel checked him out before he hired him."

"What about Delores?" Logan asked.

"She's been with us since shortly after Stevie was born. You can't be serious about—"

Logan gripped her chin. "I'm very serious. It's the fourth rule of all good P.I.s—check everyone out."

"And in the meantime, what do we do?" Daisy asked.

"We…" They both moved at the same time, and her lips accidentally skimmed along the line of his jaw. He would only have to lean forward, a matter of inches, and their lips would meet. He saw the awareness and the desire fill her eyes at the same moment. It was the wrong time. The wrong place. The wrong bed.

"Logan—"

"Shh…" Logan whispered as he closed the small distance. He simply had to taste her.

So different. That was the first thought that moved through Daisy's mind. His lips barely brushed hers before she felt his tongue at the corner of her mouth. Lifting her hands, she framed his face and tried to draw him closer. But even when his mouth pressed more fully against hers, he wouldn't be rushed. Slowly, carefully, he explored her mouth with his tongue as if it were the first time, as if he had all the time in the world.

Always before, there'd been such urgency, such demand. And she could feel it this time too, simmering beneath the surface.

Tempting her to unleash it.

When he took his mouth from hers to explore her neck, to whisper in her ear, feelings swirled through her. She'd wanted him before, but not this sharply. She'd needed him before, but not with this kind of an ache. Hunger had never made her call out his name.

When he drew back for a moment to look into her eyes, she tried to remember. It was all wrong. The time. The place. The bed. Then Daisy wrapped her arms around him and drew his mouth back to hers. Nothing had ever been this right.

One more taste, Logan promised himself as her lips parted once more beneath his, inviting him in. Her mouth held a sweetness that he would always crave. Slowly, yet firmly, he wrapped his arms around her, locking their bodies more tightly together.

It felt so right. Even as the thought formed in his mind, he felt himself tumbling into a freefall. Control, something he prided himself on, began to slip away. Deep within himself, he felt something give. He should try to hold on to it.

Instead, he slid his fingers into her hair—to hold on to her.

"Miss Daisy! Miss Daisy, come quick!"

Logan drew back instantly, lifting her as he rose, then setting her on her feet. He kept her hand in his as he hurried with her to the door of the apartment. Halfway up the stairs, Delores stopped when she saw them.

"Come quick. Your uncle...the police..." Pausing to catch her breath, Delores pressed a hand to her heart.

"The police?" Daisy asked, taking the stairs quickly.

"They're at the door, asking for you. But your uncle—you have to calm him down... It's Miss Stevie."

Daisy gripped the older woman's arm. "Something's happened to Stevie?"

"She's missing! The Gibsons haven't seen her since last night."

As she hurried after Delores, Daisy had a very clear picture in her mind of the sky cracking into little pieces and falling on her head.

8

"DON'T TELL ME you can't report my daughter missing for forty-eight hours! What kind of rule is that?"

"Well, sir..." The young officer sitting on the couch paused to clear his throat.

"I'll tell you what kind of rule it is," Daniel said.

Daisy paused inside the door of the library as her uncle proceeded to do just that. Ever since she and Logan had followed Delores back into the house, she felt as if she had somehow slipped, wide-awake, into one of her nightmares. The kind she'd always struggled to break free of in the darkest hours of the night. She pinched herself hard.

The scene in front of her didn't fade. The sun continued to splash brightly across the Oriental carpet where her uncle paced back and forth. Behind him a log shifted in the fireplace, then settled into silence. Delores breezed past her with a tray and Mark rose from his chair to help her serve steaming mugs to the two police officers.

Aside from the fact that it was coffee Delores was serving instead of tea, the whole scene reminded Daisy quite vividly of the last chapter of an Agatha Christie novel.

The suspects were all gathered in the drawing room to face the local constabulary. But Hercule Poirot was nowhere in sight.

Logan was upstairs, searching the suspects' rooms for clues and calling Ray on his cell phone. One of his operatives was following Stevie, so he should know soon where she was. In the meantime, she had to face the police alone and try to stall them if they asked to see her car.

And this wasn't a nightmare or a scene out of a book. It was her life!

Her gaze flew to her uncle at the sound of his fist connecting with the top of the desk.

"Rules are meant to be broken!" Grabbing the picture on his desk, Daniel strode across the room and handed it to the two officers. "Take this. You can at least make copies of her picture. Show it around town. The Gibsons haven't seen her since last night at about ten o'clock. That's when they went to bed. This morning they say she was gone when they left for church! Vanished! Without so much as a word to anyone! I'm telling you, my daughter wouldn't do that!"

"The thing is," the older officer said in a soothing voice, "she could be on her way home right now. Or—" he paused to clear his throat "—does she have a boyfriend?"

Daisy very nearly dropped the mug that Delores had handed her. She looked at Mark and waited for him to say something, but he didn't say a word.

"Boyfriend!" Daniel shouted. "Are you suggesting...? Nonsense!" He switched his glare to

Daisy. "Tell them Stephanie Ann doesn't have a boyfriend!"

"She's never mentioned anything," Daisy began. "I think I would know."

"In my experience," the older officer said, "young people don't always confide in family members about these things. And they'll sometimes use staying at a friend's house as a cover for meeting the boyfriend."

Uncle Daniel's eyes narrowed. "If that's true, it's all the more reason to find her."

As Daniel continued to argue with the police, Daisy tried to control the thoughts running through her mind. She recalled her cousin's threat that day in the bookstore. That she was going to do "Something that will make everyone sit up and take notice. Even you." Did that *something* involve Phillip?

No. There was another explanation. Logan would find it. He was taking care of it right now, she assured herself. Any minute, he would walk in—just like Hercule Poirot—and the story would conclude with a happy ending.

"I'll make some phone calls," the older policeman said while the younger one closed his notebook. "Make sure other sheriffs' offices in the area get a copy of this picture so they can keep an eye out for her. And, of course, all of our patrol cars will be on the lookout."

"I want her found," Daniel said.

"We'll do our best, sir." The older officer rose, and the younger one immediately jumped up. "But my advice is that you call all her friends and find out who the boyfriend is."

Daniel frowned. Daisy's stomach sank. She thought of Stevie's earring, the rumpled bed over the garage.

"Miss Hanover," the older officer said. "We'd like to have a word with you." The younger one flipped his notebook to a fresh page.

"Can't this business about Maplethorpe wait?" Daniel asked. "I explained yesterday why he might have my office and my private phone number in his wallet. He drew up my wife's will, and we spoke about it several times."

The younger officer cleared his throat apologetically. "It's not about the phone numbers, sir. The police over in Barnard's Crossing received an anonymous call. Someone claiming they witnessed the accident early Friday morning when Mr. Maplethorpe was run down. The chief there called us with a description and a partial license-plate number."

The older officer turned to smile at Daisy. "The description and three of the numbers match that little car of yours. I told them there was probably some mistake. But you know how it is. If we don't check it out, someone will accuse us of not doing our job. The easiest way to clear it all up would be if you let us take a look at your car."

"My car," Daisy said, fighting down a wave of panic. "I can't show it to you."

Both officers looked at her, their gazes questioning.

"It's not here. I drove to the Catskills on Friday and I got caught in that storm. The road to the cabin I was staying at wasn't plowed when I left, so I came back with someone else." She drew in a deep breath. She was beginning to babble. "I'm planning to go back up there this afternoon to get it. How about if I drive by your office first thing tomorrow morning? Would that be all right?"

"That'll be fine," the older officer said while his partner closed his notebook.

"What do you mean you'll drive up there today?" Uncle Daniel bellowed. "I need you here until we find your cousin. You can't desert your family at a time like this."

Struggling for calm, Daisy turned to her uncle. "I'll call Stevie's friends before I leave. I'm sure we'll find her."

"I'll be glad to help," Mark said. "Just give me a list."

"Thank you for your cooperation, Miss Hanover," the older officer said as she escorted them to the door. "We don't put a lot of stock in anonymous tips, but we have to check them out. You understand."

"Yes, of course." Daisy managed a smile as the officers stepped out onto the porch.

The younger one nodded at her. "We'll see you tomorrow then. And I'm sure your cousin will show up soon."

"Yes." Daisy breathed the word as a prayer as she shut the door and leaned against it for a moment. She had to believe it was true. Any minute Logan was going to walk down the stairs and tell her exactly where Stevie was.

But when she turned around, her hope died a

quick death. Logan was walking down the stairs all right. But she could tell by the expression on his face that the news wasn't good.

He hadn't located Stevie. She really *was* missing.

"WHAT HAPPENED?" Daisy asked an hour later when she and Logan had finally made their escape to his car. She'd spent the intervening time calling Stevie's friends and trying to calm down her uncle—a job that had grown more challenging with each phone call. No one knew where Stevie was. And no one seemed to know or want to admit that Stevie had a boyfriend.

"She'll be all right. She'll be in your office tomorrow to pick up her inheritance check." Daisy had repeated those sentences to her uncle so often, they had begun to feel like a mantra.

And she'd begun to feel that she was going to be trapped forever by the phone. Mark had left earlier, volunteering to go home and wait by his phone in case Stevie tried to contact him. But when Logan suggested that they start for the Catskills to get her car, Uncle Daniel had had a fit. She'd watched in admiration as Logan overrode all of her uncle's objections, pointing out that he would certainly want to take Stevie's call himself when she phoned.

As Logan pulled up the driveway, Daisy turned to face him. "How did your operative lose her?"

"She didn't leave through the front door. He wasn't expecting her to sneak out the back."

"He's sure she left that way?"

"He found her footprints and followed them. She cut through the yard behind the Gibsons' and then either got into a car that was waiting for her or was careful to walk in the street where she wouldn't leave tracks."

"You think the police are right, then? Stevie has a boyfriend who was waiting for her?"

"I didn't say that. But it's probable she had *someone* waiting for her. Unless you can think of someplace she could go in the middle of the night on foot?"

"She could have walked home," Daisy said.

"But she didn't."

"No." She turned to him then. "Maybe she went to the bookstore. I don't know why I didn't think of it before. She has a key. She wasn't looking forward to this weekend. She knew her father was going to make a last-ditch effort to bully her into allowing Hanover Securities to invest her money. Uncle Daniel isn't very subtle when it comes to getting his way. And I wasn't going to be here to act as a buffer. What if she just wanted to avoid all the hassle and be alone for the weekend?"

As he slowed at the end of the driveway, Logan said, "It's worth checking out. Which way to the bookstore?"

"Right," Daisy said, and within minutes they were stopping for the first traffic light in the Village.

"Tell me where to pull over."

"There," Daisy pointed. "On the right-hand side. Just past the next traffic light." The afternoon was quickly fading to dusk, and she didn't spot it until Logan pulled into the curb. "Look. There's a light on."

She was out of the car and halfway to the door before Logan stopped her. "Give me the key. I'll go in first."

"Don't be silly. This is my bookstore. Stevie's my—"

"Don't argue. Stevie might not be alone." Logan held out his free hand for the key. The moment Daisy gave it to him, he said, "Wait here until I tell you it's safe. Your word?"

When she hesitated, he said, "Stevie may be in there. While we're arguing, she could get away."

"Yes. Okay, I promise," Daisy said.

With a curt nod, Logan pulled out his gun, and twisted the key in the lock. Daisy felt an icy lump of fear settle in her stomach as he slipped into the store. She wanted in the worst way to reach out to him, to grab him and hold him. But it would be useless. Moving closer to the window, she watched him move toward her desk. The light she'd glimpsed from the car illuminated only the very front of the store, and within seconds, the gloom swallowed him up. Framing her face with her hands, she peered through the glass. Nothing.

Holding her breath, Daisy listened hard. A car moved down the street behind her, its tires noisily crunching snow. Farther away, she heard the sound of a horn followed by the click of the traffic light as it changed. Then silence.

A sudden gust of wind blew little slivers of ice

against her, numbing her fingers as dusk slipped more surely into darkness.

Stevie could be in there, taking a nap on the cot in the storage room. Daisy whispered a prayer that it was so. Logan could be waking her even now. In a moment, they would walk back toward the front of the store and wave her inside. She could picture the scene in her mind. Logan and Stevie would be laughing. She'd run into the store and hug them both.

Counting off the seconds, she waited, praying for the scene to materialize before her eyes.

Nothing.

What if it was someone else in that back room waiting for Logan? She thought of the sniper. Then of the sumo wrestler who'd busted into Phillip's apartment. She'd moved to the door and gripped the knob before she stopped herself. She'd given Logan her word.

She'd give him ten more seconds.

Perhaps Phillip was using the cot in her storeroom. He could have decided the garage apartment was too risky and changed his hideout to the bookstore. Framing her face again, she peered through the window.

One thing she knew for certain—she hadn't left that light on. Someone had been in her bookstore since she'd locked it up on Friday morning. And Logan had been gone too long. Ten seconds was stretching into a minute. Whirling, she walked right into a rock-solid chest.

"All clear."

"Logan." She wrapped her arms around him and held on tight. "You scared me." Then pulling away, she raised her hands to his chest and shoved him hard. *"You scared me!"*

"Sorry. I went out the back door and followed some footsteps down the alley."

"Stevie?" Daisy asked.

Logan shook his head. "There was only one set, leading from the end of the alley to the door and back again. And the footprints were large. I'd guess size twelve or thirteen."

"Phillip wears size twelve."

"You're starting to think like a P.I.," Logan said. "Does he have a key?"

Daisy shook her head. "Just Stevie does."

A sudden gust of wind swept down the street, pushing the door of the store open. Logan took her arm. "Let's go inside. If Phillip was here, he might have left you a message of some kind."

The moment she stepped into the store, Daisy flipped on the rest of the lights and made her way to the back. It was the storeroom she checked first. Unopened boxes of books lined one wall. Against the other was a chest with a reading lamp and a narrow cot. Over it a blanket was stretched tight and neatly tucked in.

"If Phillip was here, it doesn't look like he slept here," she said.

"Why do you have a cot in your store?"

"When my aunt was so sick, I wasn't getting much sleep at the house. If I wasn't sitting with her, I would spend time with Stevie. Or Uncle Daniel would need something. So I started catching a nap here whenever I could. Sometimes I'd just close the store for an hour or two and sleep."

"Your family demands a lot from you. Too much."

"No, it's all right. I owe them a lot."

"I'd say it's the other way around."

"That's because you don't understand. When my father ran away all those years ago, he left Uncle Daniel in a very difficult situation. Hanover Securities was in trouble."

"So your uncle has never gotten over the fact that your father didn't hang around to help out. That doesn't mean that he can take his pound of flesh out of you."

"That's not what—"

"Wait a minute. I just had a thought. Ray's still running a check on the financial status of the firm. What if it's in trouble again? Maybe we've been looking at this from the wrong angle. Suppose your Uncle Daniel paid Maplethorpe to draw up a new will for your aunt that would turn the four million over to him. And then Maplethorpe double-crossed him."

"Why?" Daisy asked.

"Phillip could have offered Maplethorpe even more money for a will that favored you. I told you before, greed is a great motivator. And suppose Maplethorpe decided there was even more money to be made by blackmailing one or the other or both of them if they wanted him to keep his mouth shut."

"And one of them decided to eliminate the blackmailer."

"Exactly," Logan said. "Now that same person is trying to eliminate Phillip."

"No. I can't buy it. Uncle Daniel can be overbearing and demanding, but he's a straight arrow. Besides, if he'd wanted Aunt Angela's money, he'd have simply pressured her into letting him have it. He's like a bulldozer."

"You've got a point," Logan said.

"And we're right back where we started. We still don't know who ran down Maplethorpe or who's trying to frame me. And I'm starting to suspect everyone in my family. You had me thinking it might be Uncle Daniel there for a minute. And the truth is, I've even started to doubt Stevie. In my heart, I know she's not having an affair with Phillip. The whole idea is so impossible. Stevie wouldn't do that to me. But when I came in the store, I hurried right back here to check the cot. To see if it was rumpled. Because I know she has the key and we suspect that Phillip might have made those footprints. For a minute, I almost believed that they could be having an affair. I'm really losing it!"

Reaching out, Logan laid a hand against her cheek. "You're worried about your cousin, and you've discovered that your fiancé isn't the man you thought he was. You're just being human, Daze."

"If I'd only paid more attention to her. She was in here a week ago. I could tell something was bothering her, but I was too busy planning to lure Phillip into that cabin. All we talked about was that magic bed. I should have—"

Logan dropped his hand to his side. "That's it. You're fired."

Daisy blinked and stared at him. "Fired?"

"I can't work with a partner who's going to

wallow in guilt. The first rule of any good P.I. is to stay objective, remember?"

Daisy blinked again. "You're making me your partner?"

"Junior partner. I still give the orders and you follow them. No arguing."

"Deal," Daisy said. Suddenly her anger was gone. Just like that. And it had everything to do with the man standing in front of her. He was closer than she'd thought. Just as the room seemed smaller, the air thicker. The cot larger. She could picture so clearly lying on that cot with Logan, his body pressing hard against hers.

Logan lifted his hand to her cheek again. He could read her thoughts as easily if she were speaking them out loud. They were the perfect image of his own. Seconds ago all he could think of was wiping away the guilt and worry he could see in her eyes. And if he touched her now, if he tumbled with her onto that cot, he could make her forget, at least for a while, the fears that were plaguing her. It would be wild. Wonderful. Crazy.

But he shouldn't.

They couldn't.

Even as the temptation grew, Logan kissed her quickly and stepped away. "Hold that thought, Daze. Until later, when we can take our time."

Then, clasping her hand in his, he drew her back out into the store. "Right now I want you to think. If Phillip wanted to leave you a message, where would he put it?"

"A message?"

"If those are his footprints in the alley, he must have had some reason for coming here. And he didn't stay."

"Why doesn't he just call me on the phone?" Daisy asked as they reached the front of the store.

"Maybe he's afraid the lines are tapped. Or maybe because I've been at your side since you went to that cabin. That goon at Phillip's apartment could have been sent to eliminate me and take you to your fiancé."

Turning her around to face the interior of the store, he continued, "He's got to be pretty sure that you'll come in to open up this place in the morning. What do you do first?"

"I turn on the lights. Then I pick up my phone messages." Moving to her desk, Daisy punched the button on her answering machine. A voice poured into the room, apologizing for a shipment that would be late. "While I'm listening, I take off my coat." She acted out the words, hanging her jacket on the rack. Suddenly, she recognized Phillip's voice.

"Daisy, I have to see you. It's a matter of life and death. Yours and Stevie's. I can't say much on the phone, but we have to trust each other. No one else. I'll be in touch."

Daisy wasn't even aware that she'd moved back to the phone, nor that Logan had taken her hand until he squeezed it. Then he punched the button to replay the tape.

This time she concentrated on the tone instead of the words. What she heard was fear.

"The machine says he left that message Friday night," Logan said.

The lack of emotion in his tone helped Daisy to push her own feelings aside. "Friday night? Why did he call here? He knew I'd gone to the cabin. And he knew I'd closed the store for the weekend."

"If he called the house, he'd have had to leave a message with someone. And there was no phone at the cabin. Perhaps he thought there was a chance that you hadn't gone to the Catskills after all. Let's get back to your regular routine. What would you do next?"

"Check my e-mail." Moving back to the desk, Daisy clicked the mouse and quickly skimmed through her messages. "Nothing."

"Where else might he leave a message?"

"I don't know."

"Are there any books he might expect you to look in? Think, Daze. Wander around. See what comes to mind. I'm going to check in with Ray."

Daisy wandered through the store, letting her gaze move over the books on the shelves. Absolutely nothing came to mind. Except for the depressing fact that she'd been engaged to marry a man, and they didn't even share a favorite book. Or even a movie, for that matter. In the background she could hear Logan tell Ray to put more effort into checking out Phillip's background. Maybe if she'd done that herself...

No. She didn't have time to wallow. Not if she wanted to find Stevie and figure out who wanted to destroy her family. She had to think. If Phillip had indeed come to the bookstore today to leave her a message, where would he have put it? Logan had said he wouldn't leave it to chance. What would he depend on her to do when she came into the office first thing in the morning?

Turning, she walked to the front of the store. Make tea. He knew she preferred it to coffee. It was one thing they had in common. If she hadn't been distracted by hearing Phillip's voice on her machine, she would have started it then.

Setting the kettle on the hot plate, she turned it on, then reached for the canister of tea bags. Phillip had given it to her for Christmas. And the folded paper lay right on the top of the tea.

Lifting it out, she hurried to show it to Logan. "You were right. I went back to following my Monday-morning routine, and he left a message right where he knew I would find it. He knows I'm addicted to my morning tea."

Opening it up, she read aloud, "Whatever you do, don't show this to anyone. I'm the only person you can trust. You and Stevie are in great danger. Meet me at our special place."

When Logan reached for the note, she handed it to him and frowned. "*Our special place?* I have no idea what he's talking about."

"Think, Daze. He's expecting you to know."

"But I don't know."

Logan stared at her. "I see."

"No, you don't." She grabbed his arm as he turned.

"I know that your loyalty runs deep. Even now you're worried about betraying this guy."

"Will you listen? What I feel is guilt. Because I

never really loved Phillip. I tried to convince myself that I did, that the only problem was that Phillip didn't love me. The truth is, I agreed to marry him to please everyone else. To pay Uncle Daniel and Aunt Angela back for taking me in and raising me. I'm trying to be objective and not to let the guilt interfere. I'd tell you if I knew what he was talking about."

After a moment, Logan nodded, then took the note from her and studied it for a minute. "He could be referring to the cabin."

"But I wasn't at the cabin with him. I was there with you. How could he call it *our special place?*"

Logan handed the note back to her. "He wrote this message on the back of a map to your Cats-kills retreat."

Daisy stared down at the paper. It was the original map she'd scribbled when she'd first called to make the reservation, before she'd downloaded the brochure. As far as she knew, she'd left it on her desk. He could easily have seen it there. "You're right. I'm letting my guilt interfere again."

The teakettle shrilled. Moving to turn it off, Daisy said, "The downside of this detecting business is that we always seem to be discover-ing bad news. Don't you ever get tired of it?"

"I discover good things too," Logan said, tak-ing the cup she poured him.

"Name one thing," Daisy said.

"You."

Just one word. Daisy couldn't have described in a hundred years what it meant to hear him say it. There were so many things she was feeling. The easiest to identify was the panic. And the hope.

When she turned to face him, she thought for a moment that she saw some of the same feelings in his eyes, before he drew himself in. But she'd seen it. The warmth spread through her.

"Logan, I—"

"Don't. Before you say anything, I have something to confess. And you're not going to like it. While you and your Uncle Daniel were entertaining the police, I searched the upstairs bedrooms. And I found some things. Maybe more bad news."

"In Stevie's room?"

"In yours." Logan drew a paper and a framed picture out of his pocket. "I found these in your bookcase."

Daisy glanced at the paper he handed her. It was her parents' marriage license.

"I want you to know I asked Ray to run a background check on your mother."

Daisy handed the paper back to him. "You're right. I don't like it. In fact, I hate it. But if I were investigating this case, I'd do the same thing."

He handed her the picture next. Daisy ran her finger over the frame as she studied the picture of the man and woman standing at the railing of a sailboat. They were looking at each other, laughing. Tucked cozily between them was a baby the woman was holding in her arms. "It's the only picture I have of my parents. It was taken about a year before their accident."

"You're the baby the woman's holding?" Logan asked.

Daisy nodded.

"And who's the other child in the picture?" he asked.

"What other...?" Daisy frowned and drew the picture closer. "Oh, you're talking about that little hand on the railing? I don't know who that is. The picture was cropped off to fit the frame. When I first noticed the hand, I asked Aunt Angela, but she didn't know. I bugged her so much about it that she finally had Uncle Daniel look into it. He found out that the first mate who sailed on all the charters with my parents had a son."

Daisy smiled at Logan. "When I was little, I wanted so much to have a sister to play with. I used to pretend that the hand belonged to her. I haven't thought of that in years."

"I found this too." He handed her a business card.

"Edward R. Maplethorpe, Esquire, Attorney-at-Law?" she read aloud.

"It was tucked under some clothes in your dresser. If your friendly, local constabulary ever decided to get a search warrant, they would have found it, along with the blackmail note."

Daisy met his eyes. "Someone is putting a lot of effort into framing me."

"You could say that. It's the anonymous phone call to the police that bothers me the most."

"Why?" Daisy asked.

"Supposing your car had been in the garage.

Those officers would have seen the dent, and they'd probably have asked to search your room."

"And they'd have found the card and the blackmail note. I could be in jail right now."

"That's one scenario. But there's another possibility," Logan said. "Supposing the person who made the call knew that you'd left your car in the Catskills and he wants you to go back to the cabin."

"You think Phillip phoned in the tip just in case I didn't get his note?"

"What I think is that someone could be setting a trap. I want you to stay with Ray at the office while I go back up there."

"Absolutely not! We're partners. You said so yourself."

"You're a junior partner. That means you don't argue."

"Fine. But partners, junior or not, investigate everything together. That means wherever you go, I go."

"Daze, it could be dangerous."

"More dangerous than a sniper? We handled that together pretty well, didn't we? And that sumo wrestler we ran into in Phillip's apartment? I helped you out on that. Admit it. We make a good team. Besides, if it's a trap, it's probably for me. If I pretend to walk right into it, maybe we can turn it into a trap of our own and catch whoever's behind this. And if it's just Phillip trying to get in touch with me, I might have a better chance than you do of getting him to tell us everything."

Logan sighed as he took her arm and led her out of the store. "Much as I hate to admit it, you're getting good at this P.I. thing. I was thinking along the same lines myself."

Daisy beamed a smile at him as she slid into the car. "I'm even starting to think like a P.I. Isn't that great?"

"It's scary," Logan said as he turned the key in the ignition.

9

"YOUR MEN already checked it out," Daisy said. "Phillip's not here."

"Stay in the car," Logan said as he climbed out of the driver's side. "I want to double-check and make sure there are no surprises."

Daisy shoved down the urge she had to follow at his heels. She was overreacting. Two of Logan's operatives had reached the cabin first and had searched it thoroughly.

Right now, one of them was parked up at the main road, and the other was doing sentinel duty in the woods.

They actually had the place staked out, waiting for Phillip to show up.

Still, she wanted to rush up to the cabin door and go in, so that she could be at Logan's side if something happened.

Leaning back against the seat, Daisy closed her eyes and tried to relax.

Only two people had ever made her feel this way. Her Aunt Angela and her cousin Stevie. She'd always had a fierce desire to protect them, too. Because she loved them.

Daisy's eyes snapped open, and every muscle in her body tightened right up again.

She loved Logan Campbell.

It was crazy!

It was wonderful!

When wind chimes broke the silence of the night, she didn't have any doubt this time about the source of the sound. It was her heart singing.

She loved Logan! It was totally impossible. It was perfect.

It was…*magic?*

She suddenly thought of all the legends and stories she'd ever read. There was usually a catch with magic.

Be careful what you wish for! She could picture the neon letters blinking over her head. This time the wind chimes sounded just like little children laughing.

Loving Logan had a very *big* catch. She had absolutely no indication that he loved her back.

He didn't believe in love. He didn't believe in magic. Or families. And he didn't believe in getting involved. The moment he solved all her problems, he was going to walk right out of her life.

Unless she did something to stop him. And she would. Hadn't she already convinced him to take on a partner?

Humming along with the wind chimes, Daisy stared at the cabin and thought hard. She'd just have to get Logan Campbell to stick around. And that called for a plan.

KNEELING ON THE BED, Logan once more ran his hands along the top of the headboard, then over the intricate carvings. No transmitter. No electronic device that would amplify sound. No wires of any kind. Nothing he could put his hands on to explain why he'd heard that sound, not music really, the moment he'd come to the cabin.

Not that he'd really expected to find anything. If there was something to find, the two men he'd asked to search the place and stake it out would have discovered it. One of them was an electronics expert.

Climbing down from the bed, Logan walked back into the living room. Nothing had been touched since Daisy and he had left a little more than twenty-four hours ago. It was the same log in the fireplace, which he'd doused with water. The dishes sat in the drainer by the sink. Nothing had changed.

Even as he assured himself of that, he could feel his gaze being drawn back to the bed. The truth was, everything had changed. He had changed. And it had all started the moment he'd made love to Daisy in that bed.

And that's why he was stalling now. He never should have let her talk him into bringing her back here. He should have just arranged to have the place staked out. And one of his operatives could have driven her car back.

The truth was, he'd wanted to bring Daisy here. He'd wanted to spend one more night with her in this cabin. And he wanted to make love to her again. Try as he might, he just couldn't seem to get past it.

But for her sake, he had to try. He could blame the first time he'd made love to her on the fact that he'd been half-asleep when she'd climbed into bed with him. And he hadn't known her then.

He did now. And if he made love to her...it wouldn't be fair. He should walk out of the cabin, escort her to her car and drive her back to her uncle's estate.

But when he moved, it wasn't to the door, it was to the fireplace. He was exhausted. So was she. It made more sense to stay here for the night. Leaning over, he added kindling and two logs to the grate. Once the fire was blazing, he stepped back and watched the flames begin to lick hungrily at the wood. Daisy Hanover had home and hearth written all over her. And he'd spent all his life avoiding those.

He'd sleep on the couch. Turning, he walked to the bedroom door and shut it. Then he went out to get Daisy.

The moment she saw Logan step out onto the porch, Daisy pushed the car door open and dashed toward him. She could just imagine what he was going to say, that they might as well take her car and drive back to the city. She knew the way his mind worked. Grabbing his arm, she pulled him with her back into the cabin.

And then the nerves hit her, settling like a hard knot in her stomach. Her plan had seemed simple in the car. It began with seducing Logan Campbell. Now with him standing only a few feet away, she wondered if she could even get her tongue to work.

Pressing her hand against her stomach to settle it, Daisy surveyed the room. It looked the same as it had the night of the storm. Except the door to the bedroom was shut. And the simple act of walking over there to open it seemed to be beyond her capability.

Everything had been so easy that first night. It was almost as if the bed had taken care of everything. When she'd finally climbed into it, Logan had been there, waiting for her.

A log snapped in the fireplace. Sparks flew against the screen and flames shot upward. She walked toward it, holding out her hands to warm them. The fire reminded her of the passion that Logan had shown her. Hot, explosive, consuming. And it had changed her just the way the flames were transforming the log. She was different. And so was her lover. He wasn't a stranger anymore. And suddenly she knew what she had to do.

"Daisy."

The moment Logan spoke, she took a deep breath and turned.

"There's a strong possibility that Phillip won't show up until morning. He couldn't have been sure you'd find his note until you opened the shop," he said.

"I know," she said, managing a smile.

"We might as well spend the night and drive back in the morning. I'll sleep on the couch. You can have the bedroom to yourself."

Tilting her head to the side, Daisy studied him for a moment. She'd known him for less than two days, and she felt as if she'd known him forever. The guarded look in his eyes was so familiar, but the tension in his shoulders wasn't. He was nervous. The fearless Logan Campbell was nervous. The knot in her stomach began to loosen.

Walking toward him, she slipped out of her coat and dropped it on the couch. "This doesn't look very comfortable." She patted one of the cushions experimentally.

"You fell asleep on it."

The terseness of his remark gave her the courage to reach for the first button of her blouse. Slipping it free, she slid her fingers slowly to the second. "That bed is quite large. There's plenty of room…"

Logan moistened his lips. "Daze, I don't think—"

His gaze dropped to her hands as she opened the button near her breasts, and Daisy's confidence grew. "I thought you didn't believe it had any magic power."

"I don't. I—"

"Then I don't see why we can't sleep in it together. I don't mind sharing." She slipped the last button free. "Unless there's a problem?"

Logan cleared his throat. "The problem is— it's—I—"

Daisy let the blouse fall to the floor as she moved closer. "Yes?"

"Daze, I don't want to hurt you."

She smiled. "I'm pretty tough."

"Yes…but…"

Raising her hands to his chest, she rested them there. His heart was beating so fast. For her. She felt the power move through her. "You keep telling me you're not a hero."

Logan frowned. "I'm not."

"Then stop trying to protect me." Rising onto her toes, she brushed her lips against his once, then again. "I want you to make love to me."

The moment she felt his hands at her waist, she scooted up, wrapping her legs around him. "There's still one problem. I told you that when I wanted you to make love to me, I'd whistle, but I can't."

"Don't worry," Logan said as he strode toward the bedroom. "I'll imagine the sound."

He heard it even as he opened the door. A symphony of sound. Not wind chimes, not chanting. Whistling. Even as the realization moved through him, he pushed it out of his mind and concentrated on Daisy. As he laid her on the bed, the urge moved through him to take her swiftly. Immediately, he tamped it down. He might not be able to protect her from what would happen tomorrow, but he could give her tonight.

He couldn't kiss her. Not yet. If he did, he would be lost. Instead, he struggled to keep his mouth gentle as he pressed it to her throat. The pulse hammering away there seemed to blend with the music that thrummed in his mind. Both were a perfect match to the rhythm of his heartbeat. Drawing away, he lifted her hand and kissed her fingers one by one, then her palm. When she shuddered, he felt a wave of pleasure move through him. It only intensified as her eyes clouded and then closed.

He would give them both tonight, he decided,

leaning down to brush his lips over hers. "Wait right here," he whispered. "I won't be long."

Wait? She couldn't have moved if she tried. Every bone in her body had turned to water. She was sure of it. But she opened her eyes when she heard a match scrape. He was lighting the candles. She watched one flame take hold, then another and another as he moved his hand slowly from one candle to the next. Soon those same hands would be on her. She knew exactly how they would feel, moving over her skin, setting other little fires licking along her nerve endings. Fires that would burn her, consume her. As the wanting inside her grew, each one of her senses was suddenly heightened. She could feel the nubs of the coverlet beneath her, smell the scent of the candles burning, and she could hear the music. Like siren songs of old, calling to her. To them both. The mattress sighed as it sank beneath his weight, and she reached out to him to draw his mouth to hers. But he resisted.

"We're going to take this slow and easy, Daze. Let me show you." He touched her then, just her hair, running the strands between his fingers. It was so soft. "I wanted to do this that very first morning when you came into the kitchen after your shower." Moving slowly, he threaded his fingers through it, gently drawing it back from her face. There was such pleasure to be found here, just from smelling her hair.

Then he took his finger and drew it slowly from her temple, down the curve of her cheek, to her throat. Her pulse fluttered. This time, as the wave of pleasure moved through him, it mixed with power. He might have talked himself into believing that he'd started this for her. But it was for him too. Because it might be all that he could have. He moved his hand lower to trace the lace that edged the top of her teddy and felt her breath hitch. She was so exciting to watch, the way she trembled when he let his fingers brush across the tips of her breasts. The way she sighed his name when he moved his hand lower. Thrilling.

"Logan, I—" She reached for him, and he let her urge him close so that he could rub his lips against hers. And taste. He drew her lower lip into his mouth and, for just a moment, sampled the honeyed sweetness before he released her and pulled back.

"I want you to feel how much you want me. How much I want you."

She wanted him desperately. Didn't he know that? Couldn't he feel it? As he moved his hands lower still, to unfasten her jeans and draw them down her legs, she wanted to tell him, show him. But her limbs were weighted. Her blood had turned thick. Then his hands were on her again, his fingers tracing the lace along the edge of her teddy as it rose high on her hips and dipped lower between her legs. Then they slipped beneath it and found her. But even as she arched against his hand, he withdrew it and brought his mouth back to hers. This time she managed to raise her hands to frame his face, to trap him there, but he withdrew again to take his mouth on a slow journey to her throat. At each spot he lingered, she felt her skin soften, then tingle.

And then he was dampening the silk that still covered her breast. Once more she arched against him, moaning his name, gripping his shoulders. He merely moved his mouth lower, drawing the edge of the teddy down, exploring the smooth skin of her stomach, the long muscles of her thigh, nipping at the pulse point behind her knee, lingering to taste her ankle.

As one shudder after another moved through her, Logan felt his own needs begin to thunder through him. The fire that he'd kept banked for so long threatened to spring free. But first he needed to see her. Rising above her, he studied her for a moment. Her breath was coming faster now, her lips were parted, her eyes clouded, half shut.

He moved away briefly, to quickly discard his own clothing. Then he returned and drew her beneath him.

"Daisy?" He waited, his own breathing labored, until her eyes opened fully and met his. Only then did he enter her. And still he fought against the urge to rush. Instead, he savored the way her eyes filled with pleasure, each time he pushed into her, the way his name formed on her lips. He would remember it always. When she wrapped her arms and legs around him and drew him even closer, he closed his eyes and poured himself into her.

PAUSING IN THE DOORWAY with a tray, Logan watched Daisy sleep. From the moment he'd awakened, he hadn't been able to take his eyes off her. Just seeing her lying next to him had filled him with pleasure. He'd sat staring at her for so long that he'd begun to feel foolish. He'd been tempted to wake her, to make love to her again in the pale morning light, but the dark smudges under her eyes bore mute testimony to her need for sleep.

So he'd forced himself to leave the room. He needed to check in with Ray.

They were making progress at last. And Ray, knowing that he didn't want important information conveyed on a cell phone, was en route and would be there in less than an hour to deliver it in person. Logan had put off waking Daisy to tell her and had made breakfast, instead.

Now, here he was, staring at her again, like some hopelessly smitten teenager. For the life of him, he couldn't seem to stop himself. He might as well have been enchanted. With a sudden frown, Logan glanced up at the carved circles on the headboard.

Not that he believed a piece of furniture had the power to enchant him. But the woman lying across the tumbled sheets? She was another matter. He could no longer deny that she had a hold on him. And it went deep.

It would pass, he told himself. Just as soon as they found out who was behind the problems she was having. And that would happen soon.

In the meantime, he had to wake her. As soon as Ray arrived, he had to get her back to the city to turn in her car. He wanted to be in Daniel

Hanover's office when Stevie picked up her inheritance check.

He watched her stir, then stretch out one arm to the space where he'd lain only a short time before. Even in her sleep, she was reaching for him.

Feelings poured through him, nearly swamping him. Fear, longing and an ache so sweet it took his breath away. He loved her. He hadn't wanted to. But she'd slipped through his defenses right from that very first moment when he'd wakened beside her in that bed. Just as she was waking now.

She sat up, and the second she saw him, she smiled.

When she held out her hand, his mouth went dry, and he very nearly dropped the tray. "I made something to eat," he managed to say.

"I just went on a diet," she said.

He laughed as he set the tray down on the floor and moved to the bed. "Me, too."

She was still smiling, so was he, when his mouth covered hers. But her lips immediately softened, gave. He tasted.

It took only the quick nip of his teeth on her shoulder to have the heat arrowing through her. It shouldn't be possible to hunger like this, not after the night they'd just spent together. But it was, she discovered as he ran his hands down her. And the moment she felt his fingers dig into her hips, she was desperate.

It might have been the first time they'd made love.

It might be the last.

No. Using all of her strength, she rolled, taking him with her so that she could straddle him and press kisses against his face, his neck, his chest. She wasn't going to let him go. Her heart was beating so fast she thought it might burst right out of her. But his was racing too.

She could feel her blood pulse at every place that his hand pressed against her. It was glorious. It was addictive. It was madness. She wanted more of his taste, his scent. More of him. So she took.

His mind was filled with her. She was all he could see, all he could feel. Her taste, her touch, her smell. The play of her tongue sent shivers through him, the scrape of her teeth scorched his skin. She was wild, wanton, as desperate as he as she ran her hands over him, pressing, gripping. She found him, and rising up, took him into her. Leaning down to him, she whispered against his lips, "I want you." Then she took his mouth with hers.

He heard the music then. If this was madness, he welcomed it. When she began to move, he lost his ability to breathe along with any slim grip he had on his control. Rolling her beneath him, he drove himself into her, hot, hard, fast, matching his pace to the music as they took each other to a place neither had been before. Her cry mingled with his as they both fell over the edge.

When he could think again, feel again, he knew he must be crushing her. But his strength was sapped. And he had yet to get his wind back. Finally, he managed to drag in a breath,

"You know, maybe there is something about this bed."

He felt her laugh bubble up. "The bigger the skeptic, the harder he falls."

Rolling over, he shifted her on top of him. "I said *maybe*. I'd have to investigate it further."

She lifted her head to meet his eyes. "You'll need a partner. A skilled researcher."

He nodded. "Just what I was thinking. And other beds." He drew a hand down her back. "So we could make a very scientific comparison."

"How many beds are you thinking of?"

His lips curved. "Thousands."

She grinned as she rolled off of him. "In that case, I'm going off my diet. What's on that tray?"

"Tea for starters."

"Tea?" She turned to him then. "You made me tea?"

He shrugged. "You mentioned you like to start the day with it."

"I do." She leaned over to give him a quick kiss, then suddenly drew back. "*Tea!* That's it!"

"What?"

"I didn't think of it yesterday when we were in the bookstore. I was concentrating on my daily routine, trying to remember everything I do in the morning when I open the store. It never occurred to me... I found Phillip's note in the tea canister!"

"So?"

"I think he wants me to meet him in the little tea shop across the street from my bookstore.

When he first started coming home with Uncle Daniel so they could work on the weekends, Phillip used to stop by the store on Saturday, and sometimes we'd go over there for lunch. He even bought me that canister. I never thought of it as *our place*. I just think of it as the tea shop where I occasionally have lunch. But Phillip has a neat, logical mind. Maybe he thinks of it that way." She ran her hand through her hair. "He probably expected me to put it together. Tea canister, tea shop."

"And you have," Logan said, tipping her chin up for a quick kiss. "You'll make a good P.I. yet."

IN LESS THAN fifteen minutes, Logan slowed Daisy's car to a stop between the stone pillars where the road from the cabin met the highway. Ray was waiting, as planned.

Logan rolled down the window. "You look like the cat that swallowed the canary."

"You found Stevie?" Daisy asked.

Ray shook his head. "Sorry. I would have delivered that news over the cell phone." Drawing a piece of paper out of his pocket, he handed it to Logan. "This was a fax I found when I got to the office early this morning."

Logan passed the piece of paper to Daisy.

"Your mother, Mary Ellen Carleton, had a six-year-old son named Matthew when she married Andrew Hanover. No father is listed on that birth certificate. Our contact in Saint Croix is trying to trace him now."

Daisy looked at one man and then the other.

"I have a half brother." Saying the words didn't make it seem any more real. "I never knew. He must have been that little hand in the photo." Suddenly she frowned. "Uncle Daniel must have known. Why didn't he ever tell me?"

"We'll have to ask him," Logan said, turning back to Ray. "Anything else?"

"Yes. Phillip Baldwin likes to gamble big time. He had some dealings with a loan shark once, a couple of years ago. He repaid the debt right away. But he hasn't stopped gambling."

"So he could owe somebody, and that person could be putting pressure on him," Logan said.

"The sumo wrestler," Daisy suggested.

Ray grinned. "She'd make a good P.I."

"She's going back to her bookstore, the minute this is over," Logan said grimly. "I want you to follow us back, Ray. Stevens and Jackson can stay here, just in case, but there's a good chance that Baldwin won't show. Daisy thinks he wants to rendezvous at the tea shop across the street from her bookstore."

With a brief nod, Ray disappeared again into the trees.

As Logan turned onto the highway, Daisy said, "Phillip's four years older than I am. Could he be— Oh no! *Please* tell me that I haven't slept with my half brother."

"I don't think so, Daze. Ray ran a background check on Baldwin. He didn't find any evidence that he was adopted." Logan glanced at her. She was staring straight ahead, her hands clasped tightly together. Her knuckles were white.

"I used to dream sometimes of what it would

have been like if my parents had lived. But I never dreamed of having an older brother. We would have been a family."

"Don't put those rose-colored glass on again, Daze," he said. "If your half brother is involved in this, he's not a helpless six-year-old anymore. Greed and revenge are powerful motivators."

Daisy turned to study him as he downshifted into the first curve in the road. "Is that what happened in your family?"

"Yeah. You might say that."

"Tell me."

"It's an old story. My brother and I fell in love with the same girl—Lucy Farnsworth. But my brother was older, more experienced, and he popped the question first. Both families were thrilled about the marriage. It would unite their adjoining ranches and create the biggest spread in west Texas."

"What did you do?"

"Nothing until Lucy came to me and told me she'd made a mistake. I was the one she wanted to marry. It was exactly what I wanted to hear, and I agreed to meet her at a motel."

"And her father and your brother suddenly showed up? It sounds like a setup to me," Daisy said.

"It was. I'm still not sure that Lucy was in on it. But after I sat in jail for a week, Lucy's father and my brother offered me a deal. They'd drop the rape charges if I gave up all claim on my father's ranch and disappeared. When I agreed, my brother got his revenge and Lucy's father made sure the whole ranch would go to his grandchildren."

Daisy reached out to cover his hand on the wheel. "I'm sorry."

He shot her a quick, wry grin. "It happened a long time—"

He broke off as he came to the first curve of a downward slope. When he pressed his foot down, the brake pedal went straight to the floor. Tires whined as he whipped the wheel to the left. He yanked the emergency-brake lever.

"Damn! The emergency brake's gone. Hang on."

He risked a quick look to the left. The guardrail offered little protection against the sheer dropoff to the valley below. To the right, a blur of trees formed a solid-looking wall. A glance at the speedometer showed the needle climbing.

If it hadn't been for Daisy, he might have enjoyed the sheer challenge of it. As it was, the terror tore through him the moment the sign for an S-curve flew by. Gripping the wheel, he dragged it to the right. The tires squealed as they spun and skidded over slick pavement. Metal screamed against metal when the fender scraped along the guardrail. The sound seemed to go on forever. Finally, the car shot back onto the road and barreled forward.

Sweat dripped down Logan's forehead. Lifting a hand, he brushed the moisture away. At the moment, the road was fairly straight, but the incline was steep. The speedometer inched upward. He calculated they'd take the next curve at sixty-five miles an hour.

"A little way ahead, there's a road that goes off to the right," Daisy said, "I nearly took it by mistake that first night when I drove up here. Maybe if you—"

"We won't make it," Logan said.

"Yes, we will," Daisy insisted. "You can do it."

Logan threw all of his weight into the next turn. The car spun to the right, then to the left before leaping forward. Dead ahead was a wall of trees.

Daisy screamed.

At the last second, Logan yanked the car around.

"I told you you could do it," Daisy said. "The turnoff should be around the next couple of curves or so."

Tightening his grip on the wheel again, Logan wracked his brain for what lay ahead. He remembered the road Daisy was talking about all too well. It was a sharp turn, shooting off into the trees at a point where the incline was steep. If he attempted it at this speed...

Suddenly he remembered. A flatter stretch of road lay ahead.

"Daisy, we'll slow down soon. When we do, I want you to unfasten your seat belt and grab the door handle. I'll tell you when to jump."

"Jump?"

"Don't argue," he said through gritted teeth as he wrestled the car through another turn.

"What about you?" Daisy asked.

"I'll try to make the turnoff."

"No," Daisy said.

"Don't argue," he shouted. For the first time, the road stretched out in front of them for the length of two football fields. The needle on the speedometer dropped to fifty-eight, fifty-five.

"This is it, Daze. Unfasten your seat belt."

"I'm not leaving you."

"You've got to. I'm not sure I can make the turn. The incline's too steep."

"I know you can make it," Daisy said.

"The isn't some book or movie we're in. How many times do I have to tell you I'm not James Bond?"

Logan saw the needle on the speedometer drop to fifty. Ahead, a sign rushed toward them announcing another *S* curve. "You have to jump now."

"I'm sticking. We're partners."

Logan jerked the wheel to the right. He could have throttled her. He would if they made it through this curve. He felt the car tilt, then skid crazily to the left. The tires hit the guardrail with a vicious thud, then bumped once, twice, before dropping back to the ground. Rubber screamed. Snow shot skyward, then fell on the windshield, blinding him.

Swearing, he wrenched the wipers on and tried to see the road.

"I see it!" she cried. "There's a break in the trees just ahead!"

When Logan glanced over and saw her kneeling on the seat, leaning out the window, his heart stopped beating. He grabbed her arm and yanked.

"Get your head back in here!"

The ribbon of road ahead pitched downward at a sharp angle. The car hit a bump, went flying. Daisy hit her seat just as the car smacked back onto the pavement.

The speedometer climbed.

Focusing on the road, Logan blinked away the sweat pouring into his eyes and said a prayer. Trees whipped by on his right. He could just make out the space where they broke—a hundred yards ahead. The engine roared as the car steadily gained speed. Fifty yards, now. Thirty. Ten.

Dragging at the wheel, he pointed the nose of the car onto the side road. The wheels spun frantically. The car tilted again, nearly going over, then righted itself. Logan grabbed Daisy, trying to shield her with his body as they spun in a lightning-fast spiral toward a row of pines.

He felt the first bone-jarring impact and an explosion of pain at the back of his head. Then he slipped into darkness.

"Logan." Daisy saw her hand shake as she found the pulse in his neck. It beat steadily. She told herself to take deep, calming breaths. The fear was still rolling inside her. She tasted it when she swallowed.

She'd told him he could make it, but for one chilling moment she'd thought they wouldn't. But he was all right, she told herself. Quickly, she ran her hands over him. There was a bump on the back of his head. The car window behind him was cracked. But there was no blood.

He was all right.

And she wasn't going to think about that moment when she was sure he wasn't. When she'd felt how empty her life would be without him.

"Logan, wake up." She slapped her hand against the side of his cheek. "The ride's over. We can get off."

His eyes opened. They were cloudy.

"Daze?"

His voice was slurred.

"We're fine," she said. "We nearly went over, but at the very last minute, we didn't. I think it was the snow. It's so deep, it slowed us down." She searched for something to say, anything that would reach him. "Your driving was great. James Bond couldn't have done it better."

His eyes cleared, then narrowed into a glare. "So help me—"

"You're all right!" Dizzy with relief, she pressed her mouth against his for a moment and allowed herself to cling.

When she drew back, he said, "If you think that's going to distract me—you're right." He pulled her close and kissed her hard, running his hands over her. Then he pressed his cheek against hers for a moment and held on. "We're all right."

"We're fine."

"I thought I'd lost you." He was shaking. He couldn't seem to stop.

"Never."

Releasing her abruptly, he said, "I could throttle you. I told you to jump."

"And desert my partner?"

"The partnership's canceled!"

"Now, wait just a—"

Logan's door opened then, and they both glanced over to see Ray.

"You're a hard man to follow. Are you all right?"

"Yeah," Logan said, wincing as he pulled himself out of the car.

"He blacked out and he's got a nasty bump on his head," Daisy said. "He might have a concussion."

"I'll take some aspirin," Logan said, dragging her with him as he led the way through the snow. "Someone cut the brake lines. We're going to find out who."

_____ **10** _____

"I DON'T LIKE setting a trap with you as the bait," Logan said as he slowed Ray's car, pulling into a parking space two blocks away from Daisy's bookstore. They'd left Logan's assistant behind when they'd stopped briefly at the office.

"We've been over and over this, and we don't have any choice," Daisy said. "It's our one chance of flushing Phillip out. If he cut those brake lines, he'll know the moment I walk into that store that his plan didn't work."

"And he may try something else."

"But he may have Stevie. And if you walk into that store with me, he won't show his face."

"I have good men waiting in your uncle's office. If Stevie shows up there at noon to get her check, they'll make sure she's safe."

"And if she doesn't show up there, we'll have missed our chance with Phillip," Daisy said.

She was right. It was their one chance of flushing Baldwin out. Ray was working on it, but there was no telling when he'd get more information. A few minutes with Phillip Baldwin could help a lot. But Logan still didn't like it. He lifted his hands from the wheel. At least they weren't shaking. Flexing his fingers, he dropped them to his lap.

"It's the only way, Logan." She managed a smile. "And I'll be safe too. Phillip won't hurt me. I know he won't."

"Why not?" Logan whirled toward her. "Why are you still defending this guy? He didn't leave that note in the tea canister out of the goodness of his heart. If that were the case, he'd have phoned you and told you what he knows. What he wants from you is money."

She covered his hands with hers. "I'm not defending Phillip. But I know he's not going to hurt me because you won't let him. You've got a man stationed in the tea shop. You're going to be right outside in the car. Phillip won't stand a chance."

She was right again. The plan was as safe as he could make it. He had to stay calm, objective. But he'd never in his life been so tempted to go with impulse. If he had, he'd have handcuffed her to a radiator in his office. But he hadn't wanted to leave her, not even with Ray.

When she reached for the door handle, the fear arrowed through him again just as it had been doing intermittently ever since... The image suddenly filled his mind. Daisy, her seat belt unfastened, poking her head out the window, the trees whizzing by... He gripped her shoulders hard, turning her toward him. He didn't want to risk losing her again.

"Daze, this isn't a story. Sometimes, in real life, the good guys don't save the day."

She laid a hand on his cheek. "I know the difference between real life and books. It's going to be all right."

"I want your word you'll follow the script. No improvisation."

"I promise."

"I..." Dragging her close, he lowered his mouth to hers. He didn't mean to deepen the kiss, to hold her so tightly that soon neither of them could breathe. But he couldn't seem to stop himself.

Finally, he drew back. "Think like a P.I. Forget your illusions about family."

Nodding, Daisy summoned up a smile before she turned and climbed out of the car. She hadn't taken two steps before she wanted more than anything to run back to the car.

"Follow the script," she told herself. Only by doing that could she protect Logan.

Keeping her eyes straight ahead, Daisy concentrated on putting one foot in front of the other. She was such a coward. What had ever made her think that she was cut out to be a P.I.?

Ruthlessly, she shoved down the fear. All she had to do was concentrate on following her normal routine. Pretend to find the note, walk across the street to the tea shop. And Logan would take care of the rest. Phillip wasn't a violent man. She was sure of that much at least. He wouldn't hurt Logan. She wouldn't allow it.

A school bus slowed at the corner. Daisy made herself smile and wave at the driver just as she did every morning. Everything was going to be fine. Telling herself that, she crossed the street and strode purposefully toward the bookstore.

From what she could see through the win-

dow, it appeared exactly as she'd left it yesterday. When she stepped through the door, the
scent of oranges and spice, safe and familiar,
greeted her.

But the man standing near her computer was
definitely out of place. When he whirled she saw
the gleam of metal in his hand and she recognized him immediately.

"Mark." For one moment, as she stared at the
gun, her mind went blank.

"Daisy, what a surprise. I didn't expect to see
you," he said. "Come in. I've had to alter my
plan several times already because of you. I can
always do it again."

"Your plan?" Daisy said. She struggled to
gather her thoughts. The man standing in front
of her didn't even look like the man she'd hired
to nurse her aunt. His features were harder
somehow, his eyes colder.

"Close the door. If you survived that little trip
down the mountain in your car, then I can only
suppose that your friend Campbell did too and
he's not far behind. If he gets nervous and fol-
lows you in here, I'll have to shoot him."

Daisy shut the door immediately.

"That's right. Now, act just as you would on a
normal Monday morning. Come back here to
your desk, hang up your coat."

Daisy swallowed hard, but she did what he
asked. Then his hand was on her chin, tipping it
up so that she had to meet his eyes. She felt the
press of the gun in her stomach.

"You don't recognize me, do you, sis?"

She swallowed again. "Sis? Why are you calling me—"

The realization flooded through her. "You're my half brother."

His hand slid to her throat. "So you do know all about me. Phillip said that Campbell was good. What does he know? And don't try to lie. You can't."

"He found your birth certificate." She watched his lips curve in a smile that didn't reach his eyes, and she couldn't prevent the shiver that raced up her spine.

"I'm going to make that bastard regret he poked his nose into my business," Mark said.

"No," Daisy said. "Your quarrel is with Uncle Daniel and me. I can understand why you're angry. Uncle Daniel never should have left you behind."

His hand tightened on her throat again. "No, he shouldn't have. I had as much right to the good life as you did. And you're right. My quarrel is with the Hanovers. They didn't want me. Just like they didn't want my mother. Neither one of us was fit to be a Hanover. But you were, my dear sister. And for that, you'll pay. Your whole family will."

"Stevie. What have you done—"

She broke off when he jabbed the gun into her stomach.

"Stephanie Ann will be perfectly safe until she makes a very important phone call at noon and gives her father instructions to transfer her inheritance electronically to my offshore bank account."

"Please," Daisy said, "don't hurt her. I can get you more money. I'll persuade Uncle Daniel to make restitution. It's not too late."

Mark laughed, a dry, bitter sound. "You're right about one thing. It's not too late for restitution. But I want more than money." Taking her arm, he dragged her to the back of the store.

SHE WAS TAKING TOO LONG. Frowning, Logan stared down the street at Daisy's bookstore, willing her to appear. The moment she'd disappeared through the door, he'd moved the car closer. Then he'd pictured exactly what she was doing—listening to her answering machine, taking off her coat, opening the tea canister. He glanced at his watch. He had the car in gear when his cell phone rang.

"Yeah?"

"Something I thought you might be interested in," Ray said over the line. "You asked me to check out Mark Dawson. New York State hasn't issued a nursing license to anyone with that name."

"Stay on it. I've got to check on Daisy."

Tossing his phone on the passenger seat, Logan put the car in gear and pulled away from the curb. The bad feeling that he'd had from the time he'd allowed Daisy to get out of the car was growing.

When he drove by the store, he couldn't see her through the window.

Swearing under his breath, he swerved down the next side street. Someone must have been in the shop waiting. Phillip? Or Daisy's half brother? He should have foreseen that, prepared for it. The problem was, he wasn't being objective.

He was about to park near the alley when he spotted it.

A van parked near the back door to Daisy's store. Leaning against it was the same goon who'd gotten away from him in Phillip's apartment. Keeping his foot steady on the gas, Logan drove to the end of the street, turned the corner and stopped at the curb.

His first impulse was to go back there, take out the guy at the van and break through the back door of Daisy's store. Ruthlessly, he pushed the idea aside. Even with backup, it was too risky a plan.

There was a better way. And he thought he knew what it was. Pulling away from the curb, he headed back to the main street. He had to drive for two blocks before he found what he was looking for.

"PHILLIP!" Daisy hurried to the cot where he was sitting, his hands and feet tied.

"I spotted him going into the tea shop," Mark said. "I missed him in your garage apartment, but I figured he'd try to contact you in the shop today."

Daisy pulled the gag from Phillip's mouth.

"Daisy, I…"

"I'm afraid I can't let you untie him just yet," Mark said. "Just relax and make yourself comfortable while we wait for Campbell to join us."

"Daisy, please. I want to explain." Phillip's

voice was hoarse with fear. "I should have told Campbell everything that day when he came to the office. But I wasn't sure. I had no way of knowing that Mark actually ran Maplethorpe down. And now he's going to kill me."

"Cut the sniveling or I'll end your miserable existence right now," Mark said, swinging the gun toward Phillip.

"Don't," Daisy said. The fear had settled to a dull buzzing in her ears, and she knew she had only one chance—to keep Mark talking until Logan could come up with a plan and put it into action. "Why did you kill Mr. Maplethorpe? Was my aunt's will a fake?"

"No," Mark said. "I might have suggested the plan to her, but she was more than eager to implement it. She just didn't want to do battle with Daniel. So Phillip arranged for Maplethorpe to draw up the will in secret. That was the first time that your sad excuse for a fiancé bungled things. Maplethorpe was a stupid, greedy man. When he saw how upset your uncle was about the will, he thought he saw a chance to extort some money from us. He wanted a quarter of a million or he'd go to Daniel and offer to testify that we'd coerced your aunt into signing the will. He thought he could protect himself by dropping out of sight, but Campbell found him. And I eliminated him. And then Phillip panicked, and I had to make plans to get rid of Campbell too."

Daisy stared at the man who was her half-brother. He might have been talking about the weather. Ask another question, she told herself as she felt the panic slither up her spine. Ask another question. "You sent the sniper to the cabin?"

Mark smiled. "That was yours truly, sis." The smile faded as quickly as it appeared. "And you spoiled my shot. That was when I changed my plan again. Originally, I thought it would be punishment enough if you finally realized that the cowering idiot sitting next to you had married you for your money. He would have embezzled it out of your account soon enough. He was just waiting for the wedding to ask you to give him power of attorney."

"Don't believe him, Daisy," Phillip said. "I needed some money, yes, to settle my account with Mark. He paid off the loan shark I was using. But he told me that I could settle everything with him if I would just recommend him to your uncle for the nursing job and help him with the will. You were going to get that money anyway. And I wasn't going to gamble anymore."

Mark laughed again. "You see. I would have enjoyed seeing you try to live happily ever after with that."

"Then why did you try to frame me for Eddie Maplethorpe's death?" Daisy asked.

"Because you interfered. I don't tolerate that. Besides, it was an alternate plan I had on the back burner all along. In case anyone got suspicious about Maplethorpe's death. And you made it so simple, leaving your keys around. Anyone in the house could have borrowed your car and driven it. If anyone got suspicious, there'd be plenty of suspects to keep the police busy. That's what I tried to tell Phillip when he panicked about Campbell, but he didn't listen."

"Why did you change your mind and decide to kill me instead?"

"Campbell was getting too close. And you were helping him. I couldn't afford to let either one of you near Stevie. I need her until I get my hands on her two million."

"Stevie." Daisy rose from the cot. "You kidnapped her, didn't you? Where is she? What have you done—"

He was strong, Daisy thought as she felt herself caught against him and then shifted so that his arm was around her neck and the gun jabbing into her side.

"You're still interfering. Before I kill you, I'll make sure you see me shoot Campbell."

THE ALLEY WAS STILL shrouded in shadows. Logan used them to his advantage, edging along the row of buildings as he made his way to the van. The goon who'd been guarding it was about a hundred yards away, gesturing excitedly to the two men who'd just driven their delivery truck into the alley, blocking the only entrance or exit.

He'd paid the deliverymen one hundred dollars apiece to keep the big guy busy for ten minutes. A quick look at his watch told him he had five left. But even as he dropped to the ground and wriggled his way beneath the van, he couldn't keep his gaze from going to the back door of Daisy's store. It was only a few steps away. He could be in there in a matter of seconds.

No. He had to stick to his plan, pretend somehow that it wasn't Daisy in there. Taking a deep breath he battled the fresh wave of fear until it was just a chill in his veins. Still, it took all his concentration to keep his movements slow and precise as he slipped the ice pick out of his pocket and stabbed it five times into the gas tank. The liquid began to drip out while he quickly used the pick to widen the holes. His first impulse had been to cut the brake lines. But if he failed to get Daisy out and they took her, he didn't want her in a van with no brakes. This way they at least they wouldn't get too far with her.

He'd begun wiggling back out when he heard the noise. A thumping sound from within the van.

Quickly jumping to his feet, he glanced down the alley. The goon was still occupied. He grabbed the handle on the driver's side and pulled, breathing a quick prayer of thanks when the door opened.

Stevie was lying in the back on the floor, gagged, her hands and feet tied. Her eyes were wide with fright.

"Don't worry, honey. I'll get you out."

How? he wondered as he glanced at his watch. He didn't have any doubt that the bozo at the end of the alley was armed. Even if he could manage to dodge the guy's bullets, he didn't want whoever was with Daisy alerted.

Logan glanced at his watch. Three minutes.

There wasn't time to call his backup, who was now covering the front of the bookstore.

He didn't believe in magic, but he wished for some now. Climbing over the seat, he lifted Stevie into his arms, then slowly slid open the side door of the van.

The goon was still focused on the deliverymen. He could hear one of them talking, but he couldn't make out the words. Stepping to the ground, Logan quietly nudged the door back into place, then headed into the shadows. Once they enveloped him, he took off at a run.

"DAISY?"

Her heart leaped to her throat the moment she heard Logan call her name. Then she felt the press of cold steel at her temple.

"Quiet," Mark whispered. "Not a word."

"Daisy, are you back there?"

He had to have a plan, Daisy thought giddily. She hadn't followed the "script" they'd discussed. He had to know something had gone wrong.

Was he just going to walk into Mark's trap? She had to do something.

As if he'd read her mind, Mark tightened the arm he had wrapped around her neck, constricting her air. Together, they waited as the seconds ticked by. She could hear Logan's footsteps coming closer. He'd reached the desk. Now he was walking between the long rows of bookshelves. He was right outside the door. She watched the knob turn. And then Logan stepped into the room.

"You're a hard man to kill," Mark said. "This time I won't leave anything to chance. Take out your weapon, very carefully, and put it on the floor."

Daisy winced as she felt the barrel of the gun press even harder against her temple. She felt as if she was caught up in a nightmare as she watched Logan do as he was told. *Think!* There had to be something she could do.

"That's it," Mark said. "Now, kick it over here."

"I'm not going to be a hero, Dawson," Logan said as he sent his gun sliding across the floor. "Why don't you just let her go? She's done nothing to you. She was only two years old when you were left behind. Your quarrel is with her uncle."

"I'm well aware of that. He took the only family I had left away from me. I thought taking the money would be enough payment. But I like this better. Thanks to your interference, I've seen the light. What better revenge than to leave him without any of his family?"

Logan laughed. "Who are you trying to kid? The money was never your real goal. If Maplethorpe hadn't decided to get greedy, you still would have found a way to destroy the Hanovers. Because you're a very sick man. I'll bet you were a sick kid, too. That's why Daniel Hanover left you behind. Wasn't it? There was evidence against you even then."

"Why you…"

The scrape of the gun's barrel as it shifted away from her temple sent a wave of terror through Daisy. Mark was switching targets. Was this Logan's plan? To take a bullet for her? Reaching for the arm pressed against her throat, she made her voice rasp. "Please. I...can't breathe."

The instant Mark loosened his arm, she sagged against him, gasping. Then using both hands, she grabbed the arm that held the gun and threw all her weight against it. She saw the flash of fire, felt her skin shudder at the heat of it. The explosion was still ringing in her ears as she pitched to the floor and landed hard, crushed beneath the bodies of the two men.

The moment they rolled away, she struggled to her knees. She could see stars, hundreds of them spinning. She shook her head to clear it. Logan's gun. Where...? Spotting it, she lunged forward, sliding on her stomach along the floor until her fingers closed around it.

When she turned, Mark was crouched over Logan. He still had his gun. Using the wall for support, she sat up and aimed Logan's revolver. "Drop it... I'll shoot."

Even as her finger curled around the trigger, the two men rolled again and reversed positions. Her heart lodged in her throat when she realized she'd nearly shot Logan.

"Run," Logan snarled as he tried to wrench Mark's gun away.

"No!" Daisy drew in a deep breath. Her hand was shaking so badly that she drew up her knees and used them to steady her aim. Mark broke free for a moment and made it to his feet, but Logan was up in a flash, tumbling with

Mark onto the cot. Phillip screamed as the three of them crashed to the floor. Then Logan and Mark rolled away, a jumble of limbs. She couldn't shoot. She might hit the wrong man.

Suddenly, the door to the alley burst open. Daisy recognized the guy from Phillip's apartment immediately as she swung the gun toward him. She fired, heard the thud of the bullet as it hit the wall. The man stopped, but he looked ready to spring.

"Go ahead," she said. "Make my day." She kept the gun and her gaze steady on the big guy even when she heard a sudden loud groan followed by the sound of a body splatting against the floor.

She remained still as a stone, her aim rock-solid, even when Logan said, "Steady, partner. I've got him covered now."

DAISY PARKED in front of the cabin and climbed out of her rented car. Only a little more than twenty-four hours had passed since she and Logan had left here and taken that mad ride down the mountain. She drew in a deep breath and let it out.

So much in her life had changed since then. She'd found out she had a half brother and that he wanted to destroy her and her family. He'd very nearly succeeded.

Thanks to Logan, it was all over now. Mark was in jail, and Phillip was going to testify against him in exchange for leniency.

She'd learned that Uncle Daniel hadn't abandoned Mark. He'd left him in the custody of his father, and he'd even given the man a generous sum of money to provide for the boy. Daisy doubted that Mark had benefitted from any of it. And the reason she'd never been told about her half brother was that he wasn't a Hanover—just as her mother had never been a Hanover in Daniel's eyes.

Daisy sighed as she circled the car to the passenger side and lifted out her bag. She couldn't change the past. All she could work on was the future. And one good thing that had come out of all of this was that Stevie and her father were discovering a new closeness. Last night, as they'd all sat in the library, Uncle Daniel had listened for the first time to Stevie's dream of joining him one day at Hanover Securities.

The other good thing was that she had Logan.

Well, maybe not literally. The truth was, she hadn't seen him since he'd finished giving his report to the police on what had happened in that storeroom. Not even Ray knew where he was.

She had a pretty good idea what Logan's plan was. He was going to try to disappear from her life.

Well, she had a plan, too. She was just going to "disappear" into this cabin until Logan tracked her down. Uncle Daniel was going to call Logan's office and hire him to find her in the morning. It shouldn't take Logan long. After all, he was a professional.

And if that didn't work...she'd track *him* down. After all, she'd spent the last three days learning how to be a good P.I. And she'd been trained by the best.

One way or another, she was going to make Logan Campbell a permanent part of her life.

Shutting the car door, Daisy started toward the porch. At least the cabin hadn't changed. It looked exactly the same, a small squat box nestled in a cluster of pines. The late-afternoon sun glinted off the windows, and a gust of wind sent a cloud of snow swirling off the roof.

She had the key in the lock when she realized that she hadn't heard it yet. The music. Turning, she glanced around, listening hard. But there was nothing. Her stomach sank.

Did that mean that the magic had run out—just when she needed it the most? No. She wasn't even going to let her thoughts run in that direction.

The moment she stepped into the cabin, Daisy knew that something was different. There was a fire blazing in the fireplace. Dropping her suitcase, she hurried toward the bedroom. Logan was there, leaning against the bed.

"Daisy."

"Logan."

They spoke at the same time. Then silence stretched between them.

For the life of her, Daisy couldn't speak. For an instant, she was sure she'd conjured him up. He looked so...dangerous. So...wonderful. He'd given her the kind of adventure she'd only dreamed about. But the man standing before her was real. How could she tell him, when she couldn't form a single word?

Was this what it felt like to be tongue-tied? Daisy wondered. She could picture the neon letters forming over her head. Before they could start to blink, she pushed the image impatiently aside. She was going to untie her tongue, and she was going to convince Logan Campbell to become a part of her life.

Why was it that looking into the barrel of Mark's loaded gun had been easier?

Drawing in a deep breath, she said, "What are you doing here?"

"I..." Logan found that his throat had dried up. Was this what it felt like to be paralyzed? He couldn't think. He was sure he couldn't move. And from the moment he'd seen her standing in the doorway, all he'd wanted was to go to her. To touch her and to make love with her. But he wanted more than that. He must have been crazy to think that if he just came back here to the cabin, he'd find the words to...

He cleared his throat. "I wanted to tie up a few loose ends."

"I see." And quite suddenly, she did. "You found a wire, didn't you?"

"No. There's no wire. I told you—"

"Then you found a microscopic transmitter or some other kind of gizmo," she said as she moved toward him. "And you disconnected it!"

"No, I—"

"You said from the beginning that you didn't believe in magic, and so you came back here to prove once and for all that this bed doesn't have any kind of special power. Right?"

Logan grabbed her hands. "Will you stop arguing for a minute and listen. I didn't disconnect anything."

"Then why don't I hear music anymore?"

Logan glanced around the room. He hadn't heard anything either. Was the magic gone? Panic sprinted through him. No, it couldn't let him down. He wasn't going to let it.

Drawing in a deep breath, he tightened his grip on Daisy's hands. "I told you I didn't believe in magic or love. But I've changed. You've changed me. You've made me believe in both. I love you, Daze."

Daisy thought her knees were going to give out. If he hadn't been holding her hands so tight, she was sure she would have slipped right to the floor. She took a deep breath. "You've changed me, too. I've spent all my life trying to avoid being like my father. I was so ashamed of him for shirking his responsibility to his family. But you've made me understand him. He gave up everything because he loved my mother, and he wanted to spend the rest of his life with her. I know just how he felt. You're the magic, Logan. You've given me back my father. If I hadn't already been in love with you, I would love you for that."

Framing her face with his hands, Logan studied her intently. "Just one thing. You're sure you're in love with me and not James Bond?"

Daisy smiled. "I'm positive. I don't want him. He's too boring. I want you."

Logan's smile spread slowly. "In that case, go ahead. Make my day."

Their laughter blended with the faint sound of

the music as they climbed onto the bed and rolled together into its center.

"Make my day!" Logan repeated as he brushed his lips against hers. "I nearly laughed out loud when you said that. I would have if I hadn't been scared to death."

Daisy's eyebrows rose. "I don't know why you think it's so hilarious. It worked. It stopped that goon right in his tracks."

"Daze, you may have the makings of a decent private eye, but Dirty Harry, you're not."

"Really?" She shifted so that she could look down at him. "Well, you're not James Bond either. You walk into an obvious trap and lay down your gun! James would have at least had some sort of secret weapon."

"I did. You."

"Yeah." Daisy's lips were curved as she pressed them against his. "And you can bet that from now on, I'm going to make every one of your days." She began to unbutton his shirt as she spoke.

"My nights too?"

"Forever. The magic we make together comes with a lifetime guarantee."

Around them, the music swelled.

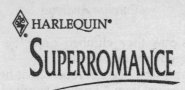

Harlequin is proud to introduce:

HEART OF THE WEST

...Where Every Man Has His Price!

Lost Springs Ranch was famous for turning young mavericks into good men. Word that the ranch was in financial trouble sent a herd of loyal bachelors stampeding back to Wyoming to put themselves on the auction block.

This is a brand-new 12-book continuity, which includes some of Harlequin's most talented authors.

Don't miss the first book,
Husband for Hire by Susan Wiggs.
It will be at your favorite retail outlet in July 1999.

HARLEQUIN®
Makes any time special ™